Tall Cedars Homestead

Miriam's Journal

A Fruitful Vine
A Winding Path
A Joyous Heart
A Treasured Friendship
A Golden Sunbeam

Miriam Joy, who now goes by the name Joy, was just a little girl in the above Miriam's Journal Series. In this book, she has just married Kermit and moved to Tall Cedars Homestead.

Joy's Journal #1

Tall Cedars Homestead

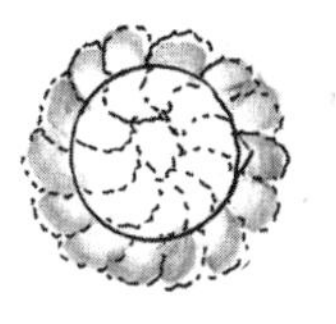

Carrie Bender

Masthof Press
219 Mill Road
Morgantown, PA 19543-9516

TALL CEDARS HOMESTEAD

Cover artwork
by Julie Stauffer Martin, Ephrata, Pa.

✦ ✦ ✦ ✦ ✦

Sketches in text
by Julie Stauffer Martin

Golden Gems are taken from
Day By Day With Andrew Murray
compiled by M.J. Shepperson in 1961 and reprinted with permission of Bethany House Publishers.

Library of Congress Control Number: 2002107564
International Standard Book Number: 1-930353-56-1

Published 2002
Masthof Press
219 Mill Road
Morgantown, PA 19543-9516

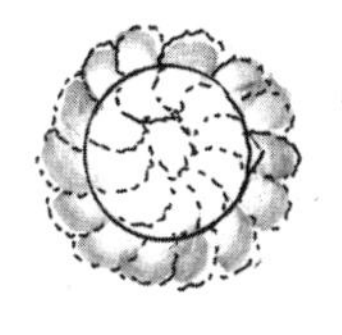

This story is fiction.
Any resemblence to persons living
or dead is purely coincidental.

Contents

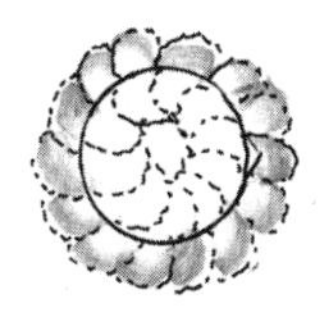

Part One

Wintertime at Tall Cedars

December 14

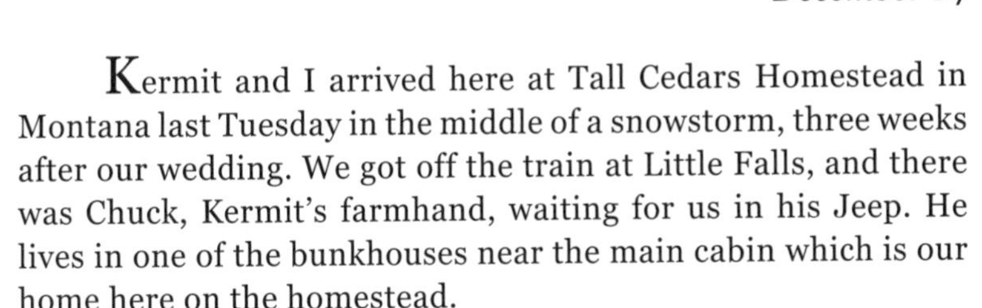

Kermit and I arrived here at Tall Cedars Homestead in Montana last Tuesday in the middle of a snowstorm, three weeks after our wedding. We got off the train at Little Falls, and there was Chuck, Kermit's farmhand, waiting for us in his Jeep. He lives in one of the bunkhouses near the main cabin which is our home here on the homestead.

Tall Cedars Homestead is a cattle farm. Kermit has already spent a year here, living in one of the bunkhouses and acting as manager and caretaker of the cattle here on the homestead, along with Chuck's help. The owner of the place moved into a house in town, allowing us to move into the cabin.

I didn't get to see much of the scenery around here the evening we arrived, since the landscape was hidden from view by the swirling whiteness all around us. We were just glad to get out of the snow and into the cabin. But the next morning the sun shone bright and dazzling on the marvelous countryside. All the pines and cedars in the seemingly unending forest around us were wearing mounds of sculpted snow, and the mountain peaks were beautiful with the deep blue sky above them.

There were about a dozen horses grazing in a fenced-in area below, making a pretty picture as they pawed at the snow, trying to get to the grass underneath. The outdoors seems so big and awesome here in the north—the sky so endless and blue, and the evergreen trees so majestic. At the end of our lane are two very tall cedar trees, reaching like sentinels into the enormous sky above.

When I come from the barn in the evening after the chores are done, I like to walk out to the cedars and gaze into the star-studded expanse above. The stars seem much brighter and clearer and closer here in Montana than they did back in Pennsylvania, probably because the nights are darker here, with fewer towns and developments.

Kermit had the cabin all furnished when we arrived. He says the house has always been called "the cabin," but to me it's much more than a cabin. I had pictured a crude little log cabin in the woods, like Laura Ingalls Wilder lived in, but instead it's a neat, homey house. There's a big window to the north that extends up to the peak of the roof. Sitting at the kitchen table, I can see the trees swaying in the wind and the birds coming to the feeder that Kermit put up for me. We see cardinals, juncos, chickadees, nuthatches, woodpeckers, and many others that regularly come to dine.

The inside of the cabin is nice, too. It has oak kitchen cabinets and woodwork, and all the floors are of varnished hardwood, scattered with area rugs. The house is simply and modestly furnished. I'm surprised at how much Kermit knew about these things and the wisdom he showed in making selections.

Kermit says our community of church folks here at the Swift River settlement is small but growing; it seems as though every year a few more families move in. Mom and Pop, along with Aunt Miriam and Uncle Nate, as we've always called them, plan to come to visit us next spring. They would like to visit some friends at Swift River, too. Now, that's something to look forward to!

Ya well, it's time to go. I have a pan of brownies in the oven and I also want to make some hot chocolate, since Kermit will be in any minute. He and Chuck are checking on a small herd of cattle that wandered into a ravine. I can hear the mournful yipping and howling of the coyotes in the distance, and it gives me the shivers. I guess I'll get used to them after awhile.

December 15

This morning I bundled up with layer upon layer of clothing—coats, shawls, scarves, and mittens—and went with Kermit to help feed the cattle in the ravine. We hitched the two big work horses, Dick and Daisy, to the hay wagon, and off we went down the rutted woods road, with Rindy, the black-and-white ranch dog, running along beside us. Just above, on the ridge in the stand of pines and cedars, we saw two deer bounding away. I'm sure they are as fond of cattle feed as the cows, bulls, and calves are!

The air was frosty and clear, and our breath made puffs of steam in the frigid air. The snow up here surely is different from the snow back home. It is so light and dry, making it almost impossible to pack it into a ball.

Kermit is used to this climate, since he grew up in this area. He laughs at me for thinking it's rough weather. He says, "Wait until it's forty degrees below zero with a high wind." Brrr! I'm not eager to find out what that's like.

Here is the recipe for a casserole which I'm making today. Kermit says it's his favorite.

Kermit's Favorite Casserole

1 pound ground beef
1 tablespoon minced onion
Dash of pepper
1 teaspoon dry mustard
1 teaspoon salt
1 egg
1 cup bread crumbs
1/2 cup tomato juice

Mix all these ingredients well and put into an 8" x 8" glass baking dish. Bake at 350° for 30 minutes.

Topping

4 slices Velveeta cheese
3 cups hot mashed potatoes

Place Velveeta slices on top of baked meat mixture and swirl mashed potatoes on top. Bake an additional five minutes.

Kermit says he likes to eat this with lots of homemade ketchup and a lettuce salad.

Oh, dear, I see three cows outside the fence in the barnyard, and Kermit is trying to round them up. I'd better grab my boots and go help him.

December 16

I just finished doing the laundry, and I miss not being able to hang it out in the fresh air and sunshine. Kermit advised me to hang it in the basement, since it would hardly dry outside. It would probably freeze over with hoarfrost right away. Now I'm sitting by the wood stove, warming my toes. The heat feels good.

Kermit was what others refer to as an "outsider" before joining the church at Swift River two years ago. I think I'll always be thankful that my parents, along with their children, returned to the "Old Order" fellowship five years ago. If they hadn't, I'd probably never have gotten to know Kermit. He came to our community two years ago, along with a few of his friends who were visiting relatives.

The first time I met Kermit, which was at one of our singings, I think my heart skipped a few beats. He was so good-looking, thoughtful, and courteous. Later, when he asked me for a date, my answer was yes, for by that time I had heard some favorable things about him. He was just simply a very nice, decent young man, looking for a better way of life than his parents had shown him. And he could already understand and talk Dutch.

It had all begun when Kermit was fourteen and his dad died. They were neighbors to the Mullet family at Swift River, and after his dad's death, Kermit began to spend all his spare time with them on the farm. He proved himself so useful that the next year they hired him as a paid *Gnecht* (hired boy). The Mullets attended our wedding, and Mrs. Mullet spoke very highly of Kermit. She said he was very dependable, decent, and trustworthy, and that he almost seemed like one of the family. He had picked up the Dutch dialect without even trying, it seemed, and fit in well with the plain people's way of life.

There are some drawbacks, of course, in being married to a former outsider. Kermit's mother isn't plain, which means our children will probably never be very close to her. But if we lead Christian lives and are good examples to them, all things should work together for good.

From our first date until we got married, Kermit and I exchanged letters weekly, and Kermit came to Pennsylvania twice a year. I visited him in Montana a year and a half ago. At that time I met his mom and she had no objections to our "going steady," as she called it. She gave me a letter to read that Kermit had sent to her. It almost made me blush, reading how he described me to his mother. He had written: "Joy is a *wunderbaar* pretty girl, with dark eyes and dark wavy hair that will not stay pulled back, with vivid coloring and shapely lips that curve so readily into a bright smile." She didn't know what *wunderbaar* meant, but she knew it had to be something nice.

I really enjoyed that visit to Swift River, for Kermit was so *wunderbaar* himself—wondrously thoughtful and kindhearted. He took me to see places of interest in the community, and we also went horseback riding on a mountain trail. It hadn't exactly been a "whirlwind" romance (by mail) up until then, but after that visit, I was sure I wanted to marry him. I got my wish now, and I hope I can be a wife to him like the virtuous woman in Proverbs 31.

Maybe I'd better introduce myself too. I am Miriam Joy (better known as Joy), daughter of Henry and Priscilla, and a friend of Sadie and Dora, as well as their parents, Aunt Miriam and Uncle Nate.

Die Botschaft came today, and I clipped a quote someone had sent in—some beautiful thoughts about marriage which I want to put on the refrigerator for Kermit and me to see every day.

Marriage is:

Loving *each other whatever may come.*
Giving *all what one has for the other.*
Sharing *the joys and sorrows.*
Trusting *each other and God.*
Forgiving *one another.*

December 18 (Sunday)

We attended church in the Swift River district, with our driving horse, Patsy, hitched to the bobsled. It was almost too cold to go, but we bundled up so that we could hardly walk, and then we also wrapped ourselves in the carriage robes.

It was good to fellowship with the people there. They were very friendly and welcomed us warmly. The sermon was inspiring and uplifting.

Kermit and I went for a short walk after we got home, when the last rays of the setting sun lit up the evening sky. There is something unexplainable about this place that awes and endears a person to it—the wild, rugged mountains in the distance whose untamed beauty makes God's presence seem so real. It's easy to understand why Moses went to the top of the mountain to commune with God. It makes me think of the song, "How Great Thou Art."

O Lord my God!
When I in awesome wonder
Consider all the worlds thy hands have made,
I see the stars, I hear the rolling thunder,
Thy pow'r throughout the universe displayed,
Then sings my soul, my Savior God to thee;
How great thou art!

Below the mountains are the gentle wooded slopes, covered with majestic, stately evergreens—Norway pines, cedars, and spruce. Next there are the meadowlands (or whatever they're called out here) where the cattle and horses graze. There's a meandering river that flows through them, which is every bit as scenic as the rivers back home, for the thickets and brush on the banks are allowed to grow wild and untamed. The rays of the setting sun lit everything up with a glorious splendor that sparkled on the glittering ice and the drifts of pure white snow all over the landscape.

Tonight, after the chores were done, Kermit wanted to go tobogganing, and so we did. It was marvelous, flying down those snow-covered hills together on the toboggan, with the wind on our faces. I imagine it was as exhilarating as flying would be and ten times more fun. Afterward we raced back to the cabin, laughing, rosy-faced, and breathless, to find that we had a visitor.

Chuck had come down from the bunkhouse to spend the evening with us. He is an older man with a lean, brown, weather-beaten face; crinkly-twinkly blue eyes; and a keen sense of humor. According to Kermit, Chuck's as steady as they come, level-headed, and hardly ever riled about anything. He's kind-hearted to people and animals alike.

Kermit had told me previously that when Chuck comes to visit, I'm to have plenty of hot coffee for him, for he's the kind who really likes his coffee. Chuck had a lot of interesting stories to tell from the old days when he was a boy living on a sheep ranch in the wilds of Canada. During the spring lambing season, the hungry cougars would come down from the mountains, hoping to snatch a hungry young lamb.

I suppose Chuck's a bachelor, but he has never revealed much of his background or personal life—not even to Kermit.

> ***Inspirational thought:*** *For a blessed day, let your words be kind and gentle; your acts helpful, unselfish, and considerate; your hours filled with loving, unselfish ministering; and your heart the abode of sympathetic, kindly thoughts.*

December 19

It wasn't until mid-afternoon that I thought of bringing in the mail, and then I had a nice surprise—a friendly letter from Mom. She had enclosed a sheet entitled "Ten Commandments for the Farmer's Wife." I thought it was amusing, so I'll copy it here:

Ten Commandments for the Farmer's Wife

1. Thou shalt not chase cows with your hands in your pockets! Husbands don't like it.

2. Thou shalt cook meals that can be served thirty minutes early or two hours late.

3. Thou shalt learn how to keep farm records.

4. Thou shalt love the aroma of new-mown hay and sweet-smelling cows.

5. Thou shalt be inspired to see the sun rise and relieved to see it set.

6. Thou shalt learn how to open gates, close gates, and guard gates.

7. Thou shalt thrill at the sight of a newborn calf and rejoice to see it drink.

8. Thou shalt live closely with God with faith that exceeds that of city dwellers.

9. Thou shalt cherish meals together, long waits for the vet to arrive, and decisions as to when to mow hay.

10. Thou shalt love lunch together when the smell of the farmer is stronger than that of the food on the table.

Lucky for me, Mom had also included "Ten Commandments for the Farmer." When Kermit came in tonight and read them, he got a chuckle out of them.

Ten Commandments for the Farmer

1. Thou shalt cheerfully leave what you are doing to fix the washing machine engine or wringer.

2. Thou shalt sow seeds of gladness of heart and rejoice to see them grow.

3. Thou shalt be able and willing to plow and harrow the garden at any given time.

4. Thou shalt be considerate and haul manure downwind on laundry day.

5. Thou shalt not be late for meals! Wives don't like it.

6. Thou shalt treat your animals with love and respect. This includes the farm cats.

7. Thou shalt be capable of fixing anything, milking by yourself, and occasionally getting your own meals.

8. Thou shalt be inspired to see the sun rise and relieved to see it set, even when the sink is full of dirty dishes.

9. Thou shalt cherish meals together, long waits at the shopping department, and decisions as to when to plant the garden.

10. Thou shalt appreciate a freshly cooked meal, brooms, mops, cleaning detergents, and a wife who knows how to use them.

We laughed over some of them, but I guess we'll try to keep these commandments, for they seem quite reasonable.

Kermit's mom came to visit today. She's a neat, silver-haired little lady and I'm thankful that she accepts me and is so friendly. She talked about the time Kermit went to work for the Mullets and first became enthused about their lifestyle. He appreciated how the whole family worked together on the farm, and he liked working with animals. She seemed to like our cabin home and admired the wedding gifts we had brought along. Since she couldn't make it to our wedding, we told her all about it.

I see that it's time to put supper in the oven—baked potatoes, meat loaf, and scalloped corn—and then I'll bundle up to go outside. Kermit told me to be ready when he comes with Dick and Daisy hitched to the bobsled. We'll go to the north field to check on a bunch of cattle wintering there and take grain and hay to them. Chuck was back there a few days ago and saw cougar tracks. But he wasn't worried, since the big range bulls are well able to protect the herd. Only in spring, when there are a lot of newborn calves, are those wily beasts a big nuisance and danger. I think it's rather exciting to live so close to the wild, where big beasts such as cougars and bears still roam. With a thoughtful, loving husband like Kermit, I don't think I'm going to mind not having any close neighbors.

I wrote a long letter to my parents, telling them what a fine husband I have. I know they had some doubts and misgivings about my going with someone whose background is not so well-known, but I convinced them that he's among the finest. He's good-natured and sweet, and if I do my part, I know he will remain true to me and to our way of life—dependable and steadfast.

Love is . . . listening to each other with the heart . . . hearing what is often unspoken. Love is putting another's happiness ahead of your own and doing so cheerfully. I want to practice that, too, and I know it will take a denying of self by and by (although for now, our wills seem to be one).

When two fond hearts
As one unite,
The yoke is easy
And the burden is light.

But love is also having respect for each other's opinions, values, and dreams, even when our wills clash, as I expect they eventually will at times. But . . .

What the heart gives away is never gone . . .
It is kept in the heart of your beloved.

December 20

Christmas is coming! We haven't decided yet how we'll spend Christmas day. Perhaps we'll stay at home and go for another long walk, exploring our Tall Cedars Homestead. I love going for walks here. The outdoors is so big and awesome.

I went for a walk this morning before breakfast, up to the nearest pine stand, and the view from there was tremendous—almost breathtaking. I saw a big hawk swoop down from a tall red pine and snatch something from the forest floor, then fly swiftly up to the topmost limbs of the tree to devour it. It was probably a hapless deer mouse for we'd seen several of them scurrying around. They're friendly, inquisitive, cunning little creatures with slender gray bodies and black tails almost as long as the rest of them.

In a blackberry bramble a lot of little black-capped chickadees flitted and chattered, and nearby I saw a pine siskin clinging to a pine cone to eat the seeds. Deer tracks led into a wild plum thicket, and I saw a little rusty-brown chipmunk, a black-and-tan stripe on its back, dart into a hollow log. Those towering pines overhead, and the awesome mountains above made it seem like a great, beautiful scene of unfathomable magnificence. The rustling of little creatures below and the music of tiny wings in the thickets delighted me. I would have wanted to follow the trail further into the wilderness, but I was afraid I'd meet up with one of those big bulls. I'm not sure where they pasture, so I don't want to take any chances.

I spent this forenoon making dipped chocolate candy and several kinds of decorated cookies and bars. Kermit will be happy. He says his mom never made anything from scratch and store-bought just can't compare to the homemade.

The weather forecast is for turning sharply colder tomorrow, along with a brisk wind. I hope the cattle on the range have thick hides and shelter from the wind. It's good the calves won't be born until spring.

I had thought of preparing a big dinner on Christmas day and inviting Kermit's mom, sister Stephanie, and his brother Brett, but then decided that I didn't quite have the courage yet. I don't know his sister very well. Perhaps she thinks I'm a hillbilly of some kind. Kermit says I don't need to feel inferior to her, so . . . we'll see.

December 21

Kermit hitched Dick and Daisy to the bobsled tonight, and we made the long drive into Little Falls to do some Christmas shopping. It was so much fun, snuggled under the blankets and seeing the snow-laden pines as we drove by. The sliver of the moon was just over the horizon of the snowy hills, visible through the bare-branched oaks. Kermit pointed out the Big Dipper to me, up in the frosty sky where the stars twinkled and dazzled brightly. It was so beautiful that I was almost sorry when we reached town, but then there was the ride home to look forward to. . . .

In the middle of the town square was a tall Christmas tree, beautifully decorated with sparkling, colored lights. It was nice, but compared to the display of the clear, frosty, star-studded sky (which is God's creation), it seemed almost cheap and tawdry. Kermit tied the horses to the fence behind the General Store and we went inside. It was surprisingly old-fashioned and very interesting with a little bit of everything, it seemed.

In one corner they even had bolts of fabric and a counter for measuring it. There were groceries in one section, housewares in another, and a corner for hardware. Toys lined the back shelves and there were novelties and knickknacks. I chose a box of stationery and envelopes for Mom (so she will write more often), and various appropriate gifts and toys for the rest of the family and the youngsters for whom they care. For Pop, I chose a pair of fur-lined gloves.

Kermit was surprised that I hadn't spent more, but I told him that I hadn't chosen his present yet. While he browsed in the housewares department for a gift for me, I purchased a royal blue stable blanket for him and had the clerk wrap it. She also wrapped the gifts for the home folks, along with our greeting card, and will ship them for us.

As we were heading across the parking lot toward the horses and bobsled, we saw a group of people in the town square. I heard someone mention the village band; they were playing musical instruments and singing Christmas carols. It was beautiful, the clear ringing notes chiming out through the frosty air: "Hark! The Herald Angels Sing," "Good King Wenceslas," "O Come, All Ye Faithful," and "Joy to the World!" We stayed about fifteen minutes to listen, then headed for home. Together Kermit and I sang:

Twinkle, twinkle Christmas star,
Wise men saw you from afar.
Up above the world so high
Like a diamond in the sky . . .

The Christmas story seemed so real as I thought of the wise men who followed the bright star in the east until they found Jesus.

Driving in the long lane of our Tall Cedars Homestead, we saw the silvery moon rising over the wooded ridge, and far off in the hills the coyotes were serenading it with the notes of their eerie yips rising and falling across the still night. An involuntary shudder of loneliness (or whatever you call it) always goes through me when I hear it, even when Kermit is close by. I suppose after awhile I'll get used to it and even learn to like it.

Oh, yes, I forgot to write that Kermit had bought a sprig of partridge berries and, in a romantic mood, pinned a bunch of them on my cape and fixed another in my hair. How sweet of him!

Love is a thing that proves itself
A thousand times a day,
In the simple little things you do
And the little things you say.

December 22

Kermit invited Chuck for supper this evening. He said he lives mostly on flapjacks and sausage and was "purty" delighted to be invited to a real meal.

Chuck had more thrilling stories to tell about the time, as a boy, when he lived on a sheep ranch in the Canadian wilderness country. Those hungry cougars seemed to keep their eyes on the tender spring lambs. His dad kept half a dozen well-trained cougar hounds, the best of which was a big blue hound named Lincoln. One morning, Chuck said, word came from a neighboring ranch two miles away, that an enormous cougar had been spotted carrying off a lamb the evening before and help was wanted to track the big beast. Chuck and his dad and a few neighbor men donned snowshoes, gathered up the hounds, and headed for the hills with their guns.

There had been a fresh dusting of snow the day before, making the cougar's tell-tale tracks (the biggest they'd ever seen) easy to follow. As soon as the hounds caught the scent of the cougar, they began a terrific racket and were following the trail in great leaps and bounds, in hot pursuit of the beast. The baying of the hounds grew fainter and fainter, and the men were left far behind. The going was hard and progress was slow because they had to stop every so often to knock the loose snow off their snowshoes. By the time they again came within hearing distance of the dogs, they could hear by the sound of their baying that the cougar was cornered. The dogs were in a frenzy of fury, surrounding a scrub thicket, and the big cat was inside, backed up against a rock wall, and even more in a spitting rage than the dogs were.

Chuck continued his story. When the men came hurrying up and the cougar spotted them, it leaped out of the thicket and headed for the woods. One of the men aimed and shot but, unfortunately, only grazed it, tumbling it momentarily into the snow. In just a few seconds it was on its feet again, heading for a pine tree fifty feet away. The cougar climbed to the very top, snarling, spitting, and twitching its tail like mad while warily watching the men and hounds below. Another well-aimed shot brought it down into a big drift below the tree, but again it was only wounded a bit.

Before any of the men could aim and shoot again, Chuck said, the big beast was up in a flash and, with one terrific leap, landed on Chuck's dad, knocking him to the ground. Like a flash, the hounds were upon the cougar, trying their best to tear it to pieces, but it managed to escape and leap to a ledge on the rock wall.

Now the men had their chance, for the cougar was an easy target, and several shots rang out simultaneously. In a moment the cougar lay dead on the ground with the snarling dogs on top of it. The men quickly called off the dogs, for cougar hides were worth $50—a lot of money in those days. But just having the cougar safely dead was worth a lot more than $50 to the ranchers who wintered their stock out of doors, and the loss of their lambs would have been very damaging to their profits.

The cougar weighed 170 pounds and was seven-and-one-half-feet long. Chuck's dad had received some raking blows from the cat's claws but wasn't seriously hurt. Chuck said that an angry cougar can kill a man in a few minutes, so it was a miracle that the injury wasn't worse.

Chuck praised my supper to the skies (the very words he used) and said I was about as good a cook as his mother used to be. He said she used to make good cookies, and he wondered if I'd try my hand at making some. He said he would pay me, but of course he won't need to do that. He went down to his bunkhouse and brought back the recipe.

December 23

I tried to make Chuck's cookies this afternoon. I thought the cookies got a bit hard and they weren't as good as Kermit's favorite—vanilla whoopie pies—but Chuck declared they were exactly right for dipping into coffee and were just like his mother used to make. I suppose it's the memories that give them flavor. Kermit said that if the cookies made Chuck happy, I ought to make some for him every now and then. I'll copy the recipe here:

Crisp Raisin Cookies

1 cup butter
2 cups brown sugar
2 eggs, beaten
1 teaspoon vanilla
1/2 cup raisins
4 cups flour
1/2 teaspoon salt
1 teaspoon baking soda
1 teaspoon cream of tartar
1 teaspoon cinnamon

Cream butter and sugar together. Add beaten eggs, vanilla, and raisins. Sift flour and add salt, baking soda, cream of tartar, and cinnamon. Add dry ingredients to mixture. Work until a stiff dough is formed; chill 30 minutes. Shape into balls and press onto cookie sheets. Bake at 350° for 12 minutes. Makes about seven dozen cookies.

I've been learning to use snowshoes, and it's not bad if the snow doesn't stick to them. If it does, I have to stop occasionally to knock it off. This afternoon I went for a refreshing walk up to the pines. The mounds of snow made the spruce and fir boughs droop, and patches of brilliant sunshine alternated with blue-white shadows on the snowy ground. I was a bit wary of the range bulls, so I jumped when I suddenly heard a loud knocking overhead. It was only a red-headed woodpecker hunting his dinner.

As I was about ready to turn and head for home, a movement at the edge of the clearing caught my eye. There stood a wary coyote like a statue, watching me with gleaming eyes, his gray fur silhouetted against the snow. I clapped my hands and he whirled around and ran into the thicket, his tail streaming behind him. Next time I'll take Rindy along on my walks since she makes short work of such predators. But I'll have to watch her, since Kermit said that sometimes a coyote comes boldly out of hiding when there's a dog around, just close enough to lure the dog after him, and when he has chased him into the woods, there is a whole pack of coyotes waiting to pounce on him to kill him. They must be crafty creatures.

I didn't linger long after that and was hurrying home when I met Kermit coming up the trail riding Silver, our big saddlebred. His whistle of admiration made me blush—he can be such a charmer! He said I could go along down to the ravine to check on the cattle, and he helped me up behind him on Silver. I left my snowshoes on a big stump and they're still there.

I sure enjoyed that ride, for we saw a big antlered buck and two doe near the ravine. They stood motionless, watching us with big, luminous eyes and then, with a flip of their tails, they turned and bounded away. Kermit grumbled; he thinks deer are eating some of the cattle's grain.

It was snowing again and nearly dark when we got back, and I said that I was hungry for mush and milk. Kermit said he'd never had that, although he learned to like fried mush at the Mullets. I'll have to cook some soon for him to try.

> ***Thought for today:*** *The three great essentials for happiness are something to do, something to love, and something to hope for.*

December 24

Our Guernsey cow came today while Kermit was at a farm sale, so the truck driver unloaded her and put her in the barn. I thought she looked quite tame, so after I had put supper into the oven, I got out our new stainless steel bucket (a wedding gift from the Mullets) and set out to milk her.

Kermit had told me he might be late, for he would probably stay for the very last bargain if it were something he needs—and the sale was an hour's drive away. I got the old milking stool off its hook in the cow stable (left there long ago) and with a friendly word to her, squatted down beside old Bossy, feeling happy that now we'd have our own milk and cream to make cheese, butter, and ice cream.

I was just gloating in the sound of the swish, swish of the milk going into the bucket when it was nearly full. Suddenly, I received a whack and went flying backward onto a pile of hay. Bossy was mooing reproachfully, the bucket was empty, and I was sopping wet with milk. I sat up indignantly and saw Kermit on the other side of the cow partition, a mixture of concern and amusement on his face (mostly concern until he was sure I wasn't hurt). Only my pride was hurt and we laughed about it together, for I was a comical sight. Kermit promised to milk the cow after this, if necessary, and to get a hobbling device for her.

Tonight is Christmas Eve. Chuck dropped in for coffee and to chat. He wanted to know all about our church's weddings and customs. I think he would have enjoyed being at our wedding! I described everything to him, starting with the food we prepared—the rows of lovely frosted cakes; the many loaves of freshly-baked bread; the crocks of pudding, fruit salad, and pineapple tapioca; the containers of cubed cheese; the hundreds of homemade filled doughnuts; the pies; all the tubs of beautifully bleached celery; the pounds and pounds of potatoes that were peeled (all ready to be cooked into *geschtamde grummbiere*); the blocks of homemade butter; the bags of homemade noodles ready to be cooked with a bit of saffron; the gallons of macaroni salad; and all the butchered fowls ready to be roasted with the dressing.

I told Chuck how all the double doors in the house were opened to make one big room for the services and how rows and rows of benches were put into place, describing our customs. I think I dramatized things a bit to make an impression and I'm sorry for it now, but it was what he wanted.

Chuck asked me if I pinched my cheeks to make them pink (since I don't wear make-up) and I told him it wasn't necessary at all, with all the attention I got that day. He also wanted to know about the services and the sermon, and I told him all about it—the inspiring singing and the counseling session with the ministers upstairs, then coming downstairs to hear the meaningful, inspiring sermon that was especially for us, along with the guests, and then standing to exchange the solemn vows, giving each other our right hands to be joined as one, for the rest of our lives, in the bond of holy matrimony.

After Chuck left, Kermit and I relived the memories of our wedding day and all that happened since. Precious memories. I'll copy part of a poem I found in an old scrapbook while I'm in the mood for it:

Love in all its ecstasy is such a fragile thing
Like gossamer in cloudless skies
Or a hummingbird's small wings.
But love that lasts forever
Must be made of something strong
The kind of strength that's gathered
When the heart can hear no song.
When the sunshine of your wedding day
Runs into stormy weather
And hand-in-hand you brave the gale
And climb steep hills together.
For days of wine and roses
Never make love's dream come true
It takes sacrifice and teardrops
And problems shared by two
To give true love its beauty
Its grandeur and its fineness
And to mold an earthly ecstasy
Into heavenly divineness.

December 25, Christmas Day (Sunday)

We attended church at Swift River, and it was good to be there. It's something to get used to: not seeing any of "our people" from one church Sunday to the next. Singing the old familiar hymns together and hearing God's Word expounded does one's heart good and gives fresh courage for the coming week.

Right after the church services, we headed for Kermit's Mom's place. At the last minute, she had decided to invite all the family for Christmas. All the family might sound like a lot, but there were only seven people—Mom; Brett (Kermit's only brother); Stephanie and her husband Kal, their five-year-old son

Hunter; and Kermit and me. It was an ordeal for me, and I couldn't help feeling out-of-place. I had to think of how different it was from our jolly family gatherings of grandparents, aunts, cousins, and swarms of children. (I miss my friends, Sadie and Rosabeth, and decided I'll write them a long letter soon.)

"Mom" did her best to make everyone comfortable, and I loved her for it. The turkey, stuffing, gravy, and vegetables were delicious, and Stephanie's pecan pie was good, too, but not quite like the homemade. In the afternoon, we "ladies" sat in the family room looking at photo albums while Hunter sat in front of the TV set, where a lot of shooting and violence was going on. He had a leather belt with toy guns in holsters on each side, and after the show was over, he ran around pointing his guns at imaginary objects, yelling, "Bang! Bang!" How can watching such things on TV be good for children?

The Mullets invited us for supper tonight. I made new friends and to Kermit it seemed like old times. Mrs. Mullet is a "salt-of-the-earth" type of person, and Mr. Mullet is like a real dad to him. The children crowded around Kermit just as if he really were their older brother. We owe a lot to the Mullets for the teaching and "upbringing" (you might say) they gave Kermit. Without them he'd probably be following in the footsteps of his brother Brett, who, he says, is "going to the dogs."

It began to snow again before we left for home—big flakes of whirling, swirling whiteness—and it's a good thing that Kermit had the bobsled wired for lights, or we'd probably have lost our way. I love snow and am glad we have a lot of it this winter, for it brightens our landscape and makes our home seem cozy. But it was **cold**; I'm looking forward to spring.

I survived the day, but I can't say that I enjoyed the afternoon much. Kermit seemed rather quiet and withdrawn tonight. I asked him how he'd enjoyed the day, and he just shrugged his shoulders. I didn't ask him how he, Brett, and Kal had spent their afternoon, for Stephanie had told me they were probably in the den watching a football game on TV.

I don't feel very well tonight, and I think it's the strain of the day taking its toll.

December 27

Today I decided to call on our nearest neighbors, Art and Delphine Rivers. They are a friendly retired couple in their seventies. I took Rindy with me and headed out the old woods road—it's about a mile as the crow flies—carrying a plateful of cookies wrapped in cellophane with a ribbon on top. (I had heard that Delphine has diabetes and has to stay off her feet right now, since she has a sore on her leg that won't heal. Perhaps it would've been better if I'd have taken fruit instead.)

When I stepped up on the porch and knocked on the door, I heard a cheery voice call out, "Come in, please." I told Rindy to stay on the porch and did as Delphine told me to. Delphine Rivers is a kind, motherly soul, and I felt at home right away. She's the kind of person one can't help but like right away. Her husband, Art, wasn't home. She said he'd gone grocery shopping and had to run a few errands and would not be back until suppertime.

I asked if I could do anything to help her, and Delphine seemed glad that I'd offered. I washed the dishes, mopped the kitchen floor, and prepared a stew for their supper. All the while I worked, she kept me entertained with stories of long ago, back when she was a young bride, also living on a farm, and of the hardships she and Art had gone through. It was quite interesting, and I was almost sorry when it was time for me to leave. She told me to come as often as I can (I was sure I would), and she promised they would visit us as soon as her leg was better.

Out on the porch, Rindy was patiently waiting, and I noticed with a sinking heart that twilight was already descending. It comes awfully early these days, because I surely hadn't intended to stay until it was nearly dark. I hurried as fast as I could without running, Rindy cavorting happily around me.

As we entered the pine woods, Rindy suddenly stopped and began to growl at something near the edge of the woods. I stopped, too, my heart beating wildly with fear. There was a dark shape near the fence just ahead, and it looked like a big, black grizzly bear! The beast lowered its head and began to snort through its nostrils and paw the ground. It was one of the big range bulls!

For a moment I really felt relieved, but not for long. The fence between me and the critter seemed awfully flimsy compared to the strength of a bull. Rindy began to bark, and I quickly silenced her, fearing that it would anger the big beast. We continued to stand there as quietly as possible, until a few cows lumbered up. Finally the bull wandered off with them. I really began to hurry then because it was pitch dark by that time. I knew that Kermit would be worried, since I hadn't even left him a note. I can't say that I wasn't afraid. I heard rustlings in the brush, and at every turn I imagined a cougar crouching behind a rock or a tree, waiting to spring upon me.

When we were nearly out of the woods, Rindy growled again. I began to run as fast as I could, imagining that I was being followed by something. Oh, what a welcome sight our cabin was, and yet I feared I'd never make it before "it" hit me. With a final bound, I leaped up the steps and onto the porch, yanked open the door, and collapsed on the sofa, panting. A minute later Kermit came in the door, almost as fast as I had.

When he had come in for supper and I was nowhere to be found, Kermit was worried and went to look for me. He saw me running for the house as if I were being pursued. After I'd stopped trembling, we had a good laugh over it. I was ashamed to admit to Kermit that it was nothing but a bull on the other side of the fence that had frightened me. But he got my self-esteem bolstered again and told me to never be out after dark again, especially since he and Chuck had seen fresh cougar tracks just the night before. I guess my fears were valid after all. Next time I visit the neighbors, I'll be sure to start for home before twilight.

January 1 (Sunday)

New Year's Day and my thoughts travel homeward. I miss my parents, remembering how we used to make lists of New Year's Day resolutions and see how long we could keep them. Sometimes I even miss the neighbor children and Teddy, our dog. I wonder now how I could have felt restless there—there was plenty going on to keep me busy and happy, and there were so many of us, there was no danger of loneliness. Here I am alone so much of the time.

It was fifteen degrees below zero this morning—too cold to visit neighbors and not enough to do inside. I wish I'd have fabric here to piece a quilt, but I wouldn't even have a frame to put it in. Besides, there wouldn't be much room. I feel as though I need to do something to keep from getting cabin fever, but what? I write letters to my loved ones back home, but that's soon done, too. I feel kind of restless and realize it's from within. I know I must learn serenity—to trust God in whatsoever state I am.

I just now thought of something to do in my spare time—make inspirational calendars for Mom and all the family back home. Maybe I can even have them ready in time for Mom's birthday. I'll make a sheet for every day of the year, put a Bible verse and some freehand art on each one, and hang them on a small dowel with a ring binder. They will bring cheer and inspiration to my family, and I'll cheer myself up in the process. And I'll dream of spring when the snow is all gone, the warm breezes blow, and the wildflowers appear by the roadside, and Mom and Pop arrive with Aunt Miriam and Uncle Nate. Just a few short months!

January 2

There's excitement in this neck of the woods, because over at the Five-Star Ranch, a weanling colt was clawed by a cougar. The men knew it was a big one by the size of the tracks. Also, two miles north of here a young pig was killed, but it may have been the work of a bear. Kermit has decided that I must learn to shoot his big Browning gun, in case a bear would come around molesting the stock while he and Chuck are out in the field and I might need to shoot. I shrink from it, but I want to do my part. My lessons begin today. Kermit has set up a target of hay bales behind the barn. I'll do my best to learn, and to do it well, because a wounded cougar is extremely dangerous.

My thoughts often turn to Brett's former wife, who left him after two months of marriage. She couldn't take the rigors of ranch life—the dangers, loneliness, and isolation. In a way, I feel sorry for her, for Brett isn't the man that Kermit is—and their sister Stephanie probably wasn't very friendly. No, I'd better take that back, for she would have just been about fourteen years old then. She's just a year younger than Kermit, and he had his twenty-fifth birthday on October 31. She must have married really young and had Hunter when she was nineteen. I'm not twenty yet either. I keep thinking that maybe someday Brett's wife will come back to him. I suggested as much to Kermit, and he told me that he thinks she has since remarried. Also, he said that Brett is involved with a woman in Little Falls. Those things depress me, because of the influence these relatives might have on our children someday. It's a sobering thought.

January 21

I've been target practicing every day for over a week now, and Kermit says I'm as good at it as he is by now. He also allows me to ride Silver, the saddlebred; he says it isn't safe for me to walk anywhere. I just love horseback riding and have gone for a ride every day this past week, which helped to cure my cabin fever. Kermit's mom has been over to visit a couple of times, and I've enjoyed it. A few times Stephanie has been along, too, but it seems there's no rapport between us. There have been a few incidents (not worth mentioning) that made me wonder about her feelings toward me.

This afternoon I decided to ride over to see Delphine Rivers again. My visits with her always cheer me up. It was a day of brilliant sunshine which made the snow glitter and sparkle. The weather has warmed up considerably since our very cold snap. I almost thought I felt a hint of spring in the air. It was wishful thinking though. There are still two more months of winter ahead. Two blue jays called from the branches of a big pine, and a flash of red and brown revealed my friends, the pair of cardinals. They depend on me to keep them supplied with sunflower seeds, and I enjoy watching them.

I was in good spirits as I put Silver in the Rivers' little barn, eager for a good visit with Delphine. Her "come right in" was as cheery and friendly as ever, and I enjoyed my visit. I helped her with a pile of mending and, again, I stayed longer than I had intended.

On the way home, I apparently wasn't minding my business. When a startled pheasant hen flew out of the brush by the wayside, Silver shied, dashing off to the side. The jolt unseated me and I flew off into a snowbank. Silver took off for home at a fast clip, and I was left standing there, alone and bewildered. I came to my senses in a jiffy and got up, knowing I'd have to walk the rest of the way home. All at once, I thought of the cougar that was reported having been seen in the area, and I began to be afraid.

Back at the ranch, Kermit had just come in from feeding the cattle and was heading for the cabin when he saw Silver come galloping up the back road, saddled but without a rider. He knew at once that something must have happened to me. He quickly grabbed and loaded his Winchester, mounted Silver, and headed up the woods road.

Meanwhile, I was walking homeward as fast as I could. I hadn't gone far when I heard a twig snap in the dusky pine woods. My heart thumped with fear as I quickened my pace. I thought I saw movement in the woods, but I wasn't sure. Then I heard a deep, low growl. I screamed and began to run, sure that at any moment big, raking claws would tear into me and pull me down. It was like a bad dream, trying to get away from danger but seemingly making no progress.

Panting and breathless, I ran, my lungs agonizing with every breath. More twigs snapped behind me. I tripped over a rock and fell sprawling into the snow, too panic-stricken to get up. I thought it was all over, but seconds later a shot rang out—and then another. When all had been quiet for what seemed like a long time (actually only a minute or so), I heard Kermit calling me. Excitedly, I jumped to my feet. I almost screamed again because there, on the other side of the road, lay a big, tawny-colored cougar.

As soon as Kermit was sure that I was all right, he went into ecstasy about his trophy, saying, "Whoopee! I got him right through the heart! That will be one less varmint around the place when calving season gets here." He flung his cap in the air and jumped up and down.

I was still quivering. Suddenly, my legs no longer supported me and I sat down on a snowbank. Kermit helped me up on Silver, and I rode home to get Chuck. Kermit was so jubilant about the dead cougar that he could talk of nothing else.

I hope I won't have nightmares tonight, for the cougar came mighty close to pouncing on me. Kermit realized it, too, and told me that after this he will take me wherever I want to go and bring me back again. How kind of him!

January 31

We had a scare last night. I awoke sometime after midnight and thought I heard stealthy footsteps upstairs. I quickly awoke Kermit, who was a bit skeptical since he had heard nothing. We waited awhile and there it was again. This time it sounded as though someone was coming down the stairs. Hearts pounding with fear, we stood at the doorway, awaiting whomever or whatever it was. Soon the sounds faded away and Kermit declared that he's going up to investigate. We lit the gas lantern and searched upstairs and the attic, but neither saw nor heard more.

It gave me a scary feeling. What if our old house has secret rooms or hideouts behind the walls? Maybe there's even an underground tunnel from one of the outside buildings to the basement. With all these imaginings, I didn't sleep so well the remainder of the night. But with the coming of the morning sunshine, I felt foolish for having been afraid.

As I was sweeping the big front porch, I saw two squirrels scamper up the big cedar tree. Suddenly, I knew what we had heard—squirrels in the attic walls! I told Kermit, and he went up to investigate. Yes, the signs were there, and now we'll have to squirrel-proof the attic.

February 2

Today is Groundhog Day. Does that mean only six more weeks of winter if he sees his shadow? I'm afraid not. Not in these parts. We had another snowstorm last week, and more snow is forecast. Kermit is preparing for the calving season, which is always a busy time. I'm looking forward to it, hoping it will be the end of cabin fever for me. Today was a blue day for me, and it was all because of what happened last night.

Cherry-Go-Round

(makes 2 coffeecakes)

3 1/2 to 4 1/2 cups flour
1/2 cup sugar
1 teaspoon salt
1 package dry yeast
1 cup milk
1/4 cup water
1/2 cup margarine

1 egg (room temperature)
1/2 cup flour
1/2 cup chopped pecans
1/2 cup light brown sugar

1 can (1 pound) can pitted red sour cherries,
well drained
confectioners' sugar frosting

In a large bowl, thoroughly mix 1 1/4 cups flour, sugar, salt, and undissolved dry yeast.

Combine milk, water, and margarine in a saucepan. Heat over low heat until liquids are warm. (Margarine does not need to melt.) Gradually add to dry ingredients and beat two minutes at medium speed of electric mixer, scraping bowl occasionally. Add egg and 3/4 cup flour, or enough flour to make a thick batter. Beat at high speed two minutes, scraping bowl occasionally. Stir in enough additional flour to make a stiff batter. Cover bowl tightly with aluminum foil. Refrigerate dough at least two hours. (Dough may be kept in refrigerator three days.)

When ready to shape dough, combine 1/2 cup flour, pecans, and brown sugar.

Turn dough out onto lightly-floured board and divide in half. Roll one-half of the dough to a 14" x 7" rectangle. Spread with 3/4 cup cherries. Sprinkle with one-half the brown sugar mixture. Roll up from long side as for jelly roll. Seal edges. Place sealed edge down in circle on greased baking sheet. Seal ends together firmly. Cut slits two-thirds through ring at one-inch intervals; turn each section on its side. Repeat with remaining dough, cherries, and brown sugar mixture. Cover; let rise in warm place, free from draft, until doubled in bulk, about one hour.

Bake in moderate oven (375° F.) about 20 to 25 minutes, or until done. Remove from baking sheets and cool on wire racks. Frost while warm with confectioners' sugar frosting.

Yesterday afternoon I made the Cherry-Go-Round recipe, which is Kermit's favorite coffeecake. The cakes turned out beautifully—two delectable-looking and delicious-smelling concoctions covered with icing, cherries, and nuts. I had made a pot of hot chocolate and was waiting for Kermit to come in after the chores were done, hoping we could have a heart-to-heart talk once again.

Well, the Cherry-Go-Rounds cooled off and the hot chocolate became lukewarm. Still no Kermit appeared. The clock struck nine, then nine-thirty. It's often late until he's done with his chores, but tonight I wanted to have that necessary talk with him. (I had completely forgotten that he had said it could be ten-thirty until he comes in tonight, since he and Chuck have things to do.) Finally, I bundled up and went out in search of him.

Outside I gazed at the millions of stars twinkling in the sky, an awesome spectacle of God's creation. I wasn't afraid to be out alone after dark, for no cougar tracks had been seen since Kermit had shot one eleven days ago; besides, I figured cougars wouldn't come so close to the house anyway.

First I went to Chuck's bunkhouse, since there was a light on there. I thought he could tell me where Kermit was. I was about to knock on the door when I saw a light flickering through the curtain at the window. There was about a one-inch opening between the two curtains and before I could stop myself, I bent down and peeked inside. There, on the sofa sat Kermit and Chuck, with Rindy perched between them, watching the flickering screen of a TV set. The sight momentarily stunned me. I whirled around and began to run for the cabin, up through the yard instead of along the shoveled path. I floundered and stumbled through the deep snow, tears blinding my eyes. How long had this been going on? No wonder Kermit had to work late on so many evenings.

Back in the cabin, I quickly got into bed and sobbed into my pillow, wishing I was back home with my parents. Why, oh why, hadn't I taken my parents' advice? Maybe someday Kermit and I would have children, and if he couldn't give up watching TV, what kind of an influence would he be on them? I couldn't imagine my dad spending his evenings sitting in front of a TV set!

I sniffled and sobbed until I heard Kermit come in. I lay as quietly as I could, pretending to be asleep. I didn't want to kneel with him to pray—I just couldn't tonight, I decided. I waited and listened until Kermit crawled into bed, not bothering to kneel and pray by himself. After he was asleep, I cried more, until I cried myself to sleep, I suppose.

This morning Kermit was so kindhearted that I felt like an old prude for feeling the way I did. And I had a "blue" day.

I know I must love my husband unconditionally, even though I can't approve of his watching TV. Maybe copying this poem I found in a scrapbook will help me:

When You Love Someone

by David Augsburger

When you love someone, you love him as he is—
not as you wish him to be
not as you hope to help him become,
but as he is.

When you love someone, you love her because she is she—
not loving in order to change her
not loving as a way of remaking her,
but loving because you love!

When you love someone, you love him, warts and all—
not blinding yourself to his faults
not denying the other's imperfections,
but loving in spite of. (God did.)

To love another is to commit oneself—
with no guarantee of return.
To love another is to give oneself—
with the risk of rejection.

To love another is to reach out in hope for your love—
To awaken love in the heart of the other.
Love is not dependent on the nature of the loved,
but on the nature of the one who loves.

Love is not dependent on the beauty of the loved
but on the appreciation of the lover.
Love is not conditional on the constancy of the beloved,
but on the fidelity of him who loves.

When you love someone—
nothing matters half so much as to accept the other
to reassure one another
to hear and answer each other
to look deeply into the other's soul and to show your own.

To love someone is to affirm that she is worthy
To bid him live life freely
To leave her with all her freedom intact
To recognize his dignity as a person
To invite her to grow
To oblige him to be fully what he is
To inspire her to become all she can be.

Prayer: *Our Father, we open our hearts and lives to Thee. Help us always to have open hearts for each other. May our love be such that we may never ridicule or prejudice the other. May our trust be such that we may confide in each other in full confidence and security. Grant us the power to speak true words from a heart of love, acceptable to Thee, and helpful to each other. Amen.*

February 3

My heart feels sore and dissatisfied tonight with a sense of failure. Kermit told me to cheer up; what happened earlier today wasn't my fault. But still it rankles my soul.

I discovered I was out of jelly, so I got a can of peaches up from the cellar to make peach jam. I mashed them with a potato masher, added sugar, and put it on the Gem-Pak to boil down; we like this mixture as a bread spread.

In the meantime, I heard a clattering out in the barnyard and rushed to the window. There I saw Dick and Daisy running from the field into the barnyard, the hay wagon clattering behind. Trying to run into the paddock where Silver was, they broke down the fence, and then Silver was free, too. The three horses took off down the back field lane, leaving the hay wagon behind. We dashed after them.

As the horses circled the field, we tried to round them up, huffing and puffing and panting for breath. It took all of twenty minutes before we had them in the barn. I then helped Kermit awhile with the repairs of the fence. Something had scared the horses while he was giving them a rest at the end of the row.

Later, trudging wearily back to the house, I was enveloped by a cloud of black smoke at the door. Oh, no, my peach jam! I grabbed a few potholders and carried the scorched kettle out to the back yard. The remainder of the peach and sugar mixture was reduced to ashes—a sorry sight.

I hurried to open all the doors and windows to let out the smoke; it was then that I saw a carriage coming in the lane. Of all times, what an inappropriate time to have visitors! I knew there was nothing to do but invite them in, since it would never do to tell them to go home and come back at a better time. I was hoping it might be just a neighbor man coming to borrow a tool from Kermit but no. . . . A woman wearing a bonnet was getting out of the carriage and starting in the walk. Oh, well, I told myself, grin and bear it. Smile and be serene as though nothing were wrong.

When I realized the visitors were the Manuels of the west end, my courage failed me. They are the most prim and proper couple in our district. She always has her house and yard spotlessly spic and span and is always the first to have her housecleaning done, and doesn't hesitate to make it known. She has a ready tongue, too, talking about others who can't manage as well. Oh, dear! But I survived the visit. She was quite friendly and understanding. And guess what she brought! A jar of grape jelly—just what we needed!

I still felt like a failure for not setting the kettle off the stove before I ran out to help, but Kermit made light of it and said some nice things to make me feel better. My friend Sadie has a motto in her room that says: *Love is not tearing down, but building up with loving words and actions.* That must be true!

February 4

An amusing thing happened today. Not long ago, a man in a rattly, old pickup had come and said he would file the horses' teeth. Kermit knew that it was necessary to have it done but thought his price—$40 for each horse—was a bit high. Because it had to be done, he told him to go ahead.

Today this same man drove in the lane, apparently forgetting that he had already been here. He came while we were eating dinner. This time he came to the side door, asking if it was necessary to have our horses' teeth filed. Kermit was amused and told him to go out to the barn and check, and if it was necessary, to go ahead and file them.

Awhile later the man came back to the house and presented us with a bill, saying it was very necessary. It was then that Kermit showed him last week's bill and told him he had just done it. The man turned red in the face and, without another word, quickly left with his bill. He must be getting old and forgetful or else he thinks Kermit must be mighty dumb. *Ei yi yi!*

I had a letter from my friend Rachel. She was married the same month we were and now has a secret to tell. I won't even write it in here, though. I'm feeling too envious. I wish it was me! But I'll try to be patient and accept my lot in life as God wills it. Rachel sent me a sheet with "Ten Commandments for Wives" on it, and on the back was "Ten Commandments for Husbands." I'll copy them here:

Ten Commandments for Wives

1. Honor thy womanhood that thy days may be long in the house which thy husband provideth for thee.

2. Expect not thy husband to give thee as many luxuries as thy father hath given thee after many years of hard labor and economies.

3. Forget not the virtue of good humor, for, verily, all that a man hath will he give for a woman's smile.

4. Thou shalt not nag.

5. Thou shalt coddle thy husband, for, verily, every man loveth to be fussed over.

6. Remember that the frank approval of thy husband is worth more to thee than the sidelong glances of many strangers.

7. Forget not the grace of cleanliness and good dressing.

8. Permit no one to assure thee that thou art having a hard time of it, neither thy mother, nor thy sister, nor thy maiden aunt, nor any of thy kinsfolk, for the judge will not hold her guiltless who letteth another disparage her husband.

9. Keep thy home with all diligence, for out of it cometh the joys of thine old age.

10. Commit thy ways unto the Lord thy God, and thy children shall rise up and call thee blessed.

Good advice to my way of thinking, and now here are some commandments for Kermit:

Ten Commandments for Husbands

1. Remember that thy wife is thy partner and not thy property.

2. Do not expect thy wife to be thy wife and thy wage earner at the same time.
3. Think not that thy business is none of thy wife's business.

4. Thou shalt hold thy wife's love by the same means that thou didst win it.

5. Thou shalt make the building of thy home thy first business.

6. Thou shalt cooperate with thy wife in establishing family discipline.

7. Thou shalt enter into thy house with cheerfulness.

8. Thou shalt not let anyone criticize thy wife to thy face and get away with it, neither thy father, nor thy mother, nor thy brethren, nor thy relatives.

9. Thou shalt not take thy wife for granted.

10. Remember thy home, to keep it holy.

Kermit was thoughtful as he read these commandments and said he would do his best to keep them. I want to do the same.

Thought for today: *Love . . .*
is a gift to be shared forever!

February 6

Today I made doughnuts—heaps and heaps of the yummy, delicious, powdered cakes. It was the first time I tried my hand at making so many alone, but all went well. Kermit and Chuck simply raved over them. Kermit had invited Chuck to the house to visit, so I made a pot of coffee to serve with the doughnuts, and Chuck lingered awhile to visit. He surely is a friendly, good-natured chap.

When Chuck got up to leave, he said he has a few errands to do in Little Falls, and he said if we needed anything, we were welcome to ride along. That was when I got the notion to go along and visit Kermit's mom and take her some fresh doughnuts. That ought to make her happy, I figured. She lives in a small bungalow on the outskirts of town, surrounded by a small fenced-in yard. She wasn't home, so I guess we'll have to try another day.

I milked Bossy the cow again this morning. (I was determined to not let her get the best of me.) I was real firm with her and she took the hint. She was as meek as she could be. When I came in with the milk, Kermit had already set the table for breakfast and was frying eggs. He had a puzzled look on his face and said, "Something's the matter with these eggs. They're sticking to the pan and they don't look right."

I asked him if he put butter in the frying pan, and he said, "No. I used the margarine in this yellow container." When I checked it out, I discovered that he had used butter cream frosting instead, thinking it was soft margarine. It was funny to me, but he looked so woebegone, I tried not to laugh. (That's what I get for buying ready-to-eat frosting instead of making it from scratch.) I told him I was grateful for his helpfulness, and that he's the best and dearest husband anyone could wish for, and I meant every word.

We had visitors again today—two older ladies who were born in this house and had lived here until they were in their thirties. My, what a lot of memories this place holds for them. They were very dear and gentle ladies, but they must have been young and rambunctious at one time, according to the tales they told.

They used to slide down the bannister of the open stairway, and they had built a treehouse in the big oak tree in the back yard. They had nailed wooden blocks to the trunk of the tree for steps, and those blocks are still there, although the tree house isn't. Kermit said they must have used blocks of cedar wood, or else they'd have rotted away long ago. Out against the barn there's a ring with a chain attached to it where the oldest sister's boyfriend tied his horse when he came to see her, so either they were plain then, too, or else it was before the time of cars. They had a lot to say about this Tall Cedars Homestead and its many trees and ridges.

This farm is just right for us. Wouldn't it be nice if we could buy it and stay here to raise our family? But, it's not possible, even if we could afford it, so it's no use wishing. Dreaming about it won't hurt, I suppose.

Tonight Kermit and I went for a walk up to the ridge. While we were there, he confessed to me that he had been watching TV but intends to quit. That brought tears to my eyes—tears of joy! I told him how happy it made me.

We stood under two big cedars for awhile, listening to the wind sighing through the branches—a soothing sound. The moon was rising and the coyotes were howling in the distance.

February 8

I mixed a batch of bread dough, and it turned out beautiful and light, probably because I didn't add much whole wheat flour. Kermit thought it was the best he had ever eaten! I also tried my hand at making cinnamon buns, and they turned out beautifully, too. I frosted them with homemade frosting, covered them with a dish towel, and set them on the pantry shelf where it's cool.

At dinner I proudly carried in the pan of delectable buns and set them in front of Kermit. With a flourish, I whisked off the towel and, to my horror, a mouse jumped out of the pan, ran down the table leg, and disappeared underneath the stove! The cinnamon buns were nibbled and spoiled. What a disappointment!

It must be true: pride goeth before a fall. Maybe I was a bit too proud of my success. Kermit said it doesn't matter, and that it wasn't my fault. Oh, well, I'll make more . . . for . . . "Love is the joy of doing things for someone dear to you."

Tonight Kermit baited two mousetraps with cheese and set one in back of the stove and one between the wall and refrigerator.

February 10

Yesterday a young couple with a baby stopped in here, sent by their friends, Stephanie and Kal. They said they need a babysitter for a few days while they go on a mini-vacation. Shana, their three-month-old daughter, has colic and is quite fussy. They felt they just simply needed a break. She was a pretty little thing, cooing and kicking in her carrier, the picture of sweetness and innocence. Of course, we said we'd love to have her. I figured maybe the young mother just didn't know much about handling a baby, and she would be very *brauuv* (contented) for me.

Shana arrived this morning, still in her pink bunny sleeper, looking very cuddly and lovable. Kermit was nearly as delighted as I was. What fun to have a sweet baby in the house! For awhile she did just fine, seeming to like it when I rocked her in the big Boston rocker. When she started to become *grittlich* (fussy), I fed her a bottle of formula. It was such a satisfying feeling to feed her and she took it nicely. But it didn't last long and soon the "fun" began!

Shana pulled up her little legs, became red in the face, and simply yelled. Kermit took his turn walking the floor with her, and though we rocked and patted her until we were exhausted, it was all to no avail. Chuck even came in and took a turn. We were so concerned, we forgot that it was dinnertime. The baby cried and cried, and I could have cried with her.

Soon we saw a carriage coming in the lane. Oh, joy! It was the Mullets. Surely Mrs. Mullet would know what to do, and I could hand the responsibility over to her. Taking in the situation, Mrs. Mullet calmly began to brew a pot of *katza graut* (catnip tea). After it was ready and cooled to lukewarm, she gave it to little Shana in her bottle. Either it had magical healing powers, or else the colic attack had run its course, for the baby was soon peacefully sleeping. I wondered how the Mullets knew we needed them. Mrs. Mullet said they had been planning for awhile to hitch up and come over for a long overdue visit.

Kermit is holding Shana now, and a lovely picture it makes indeed. She's at her sweetest now, and the old longing is back when I see him holding her. When she's happy like this, he hovers around her, trying to get her to gurgle and coo. I can't help imagine what it will be like when the child he is holding and the one on his knee is our very own to love and cherish.

Golden Gem for today: *Holiness is not something we do or attain; it is the communication of the divine life, the inbreathing of the Divine nature, the power of the Divine presence resting on us.*

We had a letter from my mom today and it gave me a bit of *zeitlang* (homesickness), I think. Mom wrote that they were having a very mild and balmy week—so mild that a fire in the big kitchen range was hardly necessary. (It's hard to imagine it being that mild here, this time of year.) She mentioned that on the evening she was writing this letter, Sis was sewing new curtains for her bedroom; the little ones were building a cabin out of Lego blocks; the middle ones were playing Scrabble; the older ones were working on various projects; and Pop was reading the newspaper. I can just imagine their pleasant, cheery kitchen, with the teakettle humming on the stove, a bowl of popcorn being passed around, and someone starting a song with the rest joining in.

Here it is nearly zero degrees, the coyotes are howling their evening serenade, and the wind is sighing in the cedars. Kermit and Chuck have just come in from the field where they were checking the cattle. I guess I'll fill a sheet for the family right now, and ask Kermit to fill the other side. Dad won't be able to come along to visit us this spring, so we'll have to be satisfied with reading about him in their letters. But the great news—Mom is coming soon! She'll be here when calving season is over, along with Aunt Miriam and Uncle Nate. I can hardly wait!

I also received a letter from Sadie. She sent me the following poem about love, but she writes that there are many kinds of love besides romantic love, which is sometimes the kind young people mostly think about.

Love is a power
That transforms the soul,
Fills hearts with heaven
And gives life its goal.

Love is an attitude
Love is a prayer
For a soul in sorrow
A heart in despair.

Love is good wishes
For the gain of another,
Love suffers long
With the faults of a brother.

Love gives water to
A cup that's run dry,

Love reaches low
As it reaches high.

Seeks not her own
At expense of another,
Love reaches God
When it reaches brother.

Right now, Shana is stirring and yawning. I need to get another bottle ready. Maybe this session of babysitting will do me a lot of good when the longing for a baby of our own gives me heartaches again. I'm sure they're worth every tired bone, and that the heartache of childlessness would be greater than the amount of cares and responsibilities they bring with them.

February 12 (Sunday)

We attended church services this morning, and tonight Art and Delphine came over. They kept us royally entertained with stories of long ago, and we listened with rapt attention. They talked of bygone years, of how their grandparents had to scrimp and save to keep food on the table for a houseful of growing of children. They had fried mush for breakfast, as much as they wanted, and oatmeal with milk, and not much else.

The Rivers are an interesting older couple, and I hope that when spring comes, we'll get to know more of our neighbors.

Shana goes home tonight, and I guess I'll have to admit it will be somewhat of a relief to hand her over to her parents, even though she does fairly well on catnip tea. I guess I just didn't realize that caring for a baby is such a responsibility, and that it's not all joy.

Oh, oh, I see one of our range bulls out on the driveway, snorting and pawing. I must tell Kermit and Chuck.

March 11

The Herefords have begun to calve. It's an interesting time, if you can call getting up several times each night to check on the cows exciting. I always get dressed and go along out, too, thinking I might be able to be of some help. We were hoping for milder weather during calving time, but this morning it was nine degrees below zero! What a cold world for these babies to he ushered into.

The cows have to be watched closely, and if any show signs of calving, they are quickly chased into the warm barn. The calves wouldn't have much of a chance out in the sub-zero weather for any length of time.

Last night, a group of cows huddled in the fir grove behind the barn. I went along to check on them. The moon dazzled brightly on the crisp snow and everything was already covered with white hoarfrost. What a beautiful sight! Two of the cows were in labor, and with a lot of coaxing and shoving, we finally had them separated from the rest of the herd and headed for the barn. Our breath was like clouds of smoke, but I was toasty warm from exertion. Besides, I was bundled up in so many layers of clothing, I don't think I'd have felt anything if I'd have fallen.

By two o'clock this morning a nice heifer calf had safely arrived, and she was a lively one, able to start nursing without much help at all. Kermit said that calving time would be a pleasure if they were all like that. Chuck arrived then to take his turn at watching the cows and we went back to bed.

At six o'clock we were heading for the barn again when we saw Chuck hurrying up from the grove, half carrying and half dragging a newborn calf. One of the other cows had unexpectedly dropped a calf out in the open, and it was already partially frozen.

"Hurry!" Chuck shouted, panting from the exertion. "Into my bunkhouse, and get the warm water running in the tub." They rubbed and rubbed him, but all to no avail, for there were no signs of life. Too late.

Back to the herd. Yes, another cow shows signs of calving. Into the barn quickly before we lose another one. So it went, for there's never a dull moment during calving time; the cows have to be watched around the clock. Before long, there will be more than one hundred new calves in the barn with their mamas, and the hectic calving time will be over for another year. There's one good thing about it . . . there's no time to brood over other things. All other emotions (such as homesickness) are pushed aside. We sleep when we get the chance and we're thankful for it. All else pales in significance.

March 14

With all the new little calves starting to frisk about, there's a new worry plaguing the ranchers. A big bear is in the vicinity, and he's lean and mean, just out of hibernation. We think he came down from Canada, because there was an extra severe winter up there and a lack of food in the woods. Chuck said that the bear would be liable to eat anything that crossed his path—anything that would satisfy his ravenous hunger. He killed a shoat on a ranch a few miles north of here and was last seen heading this way. I surely hope they track him down soon, for as dangerous as the beast is, it's not safe for anyone to be far from the buildings, even in broad daylight. I've been brushing up on firing Kermit's Browning, for who knows, I might need it sometime.

This evening, there was a beautiful sunset behind the dark pine ridge in the west—the most gorgeous one I'd ever seen, I believe. I was just about to head for the barn to help feed the cows that calved and are indoors when a four-wheeler came roaring down the back woods road. On it were two men from the Five-Star Ranch. They said they'd seen the mean brute of a bear near their ranch and had come for help in tracking him down.

Kermit quickly got his Winchester (leaving the Browning for me) and Chuck took his old Savage, and off they roared in hot pursuit. I continued to do the chores alone and was about half done when they returned. They had had no luck; the bear had simply disappeared, and it was too dark to continue tracking. But

tomorrow they plan to resume their hunt with renewed vigor, determined to get him at all costs. I'm praying they will.

March 15

Early this morning after the chores were done and the sun was up, the men resumed the bear hunt where they'd left off last night. Kermit warned me to have the Browning loaded and ready and to be on the alert in case the bear circles back this way. Bears have been known to tear off locked barn doors to get at the helpless animals inside.

The day passed quietly and uneventfully, and as twilight approached I was eagerly awaiting the return of the men. I decided to begin the chores, being careful to take the loaded Browning with me wherever I went. I wasn't taking any chances. By the time I had the horses fed, the sun was slipping down behind the pine hills and the sky was aglow with another unforgettable sunset.

I locked the barn door securely, then headed for the cow barn. There I lit a lantern and hung it on a beam above the feed entry. An uneasy feeling assailed me; I glanced nervously out the window. I could hear Dick and Daisy stomping and kicking in their stalls and Silver and Patsy whinnied uneasily. Even the cows were beginning to become nervous, lowing restlessly and milling into the corners.

With the gun ready, I slowly opened the barn door and peeked out. All seemed to be all right there, until I glanced down at the ground. There, in the fresh snow, were the tracks of a bear! I knew it had to be a big one, the way the tracks were sunk into the snow. Tense and quivering with excitement, I slowly raised the Browning. The bear might be just around the corner and could be at the door in a matter of seconds. Quivering with fear, I tried to steady myself so I could aim straight. By then I could hear the horses plunging and rearing in their stalls, and Silver neighed a shrill high scream of fear. Slowly, as if in a dream, I took a few steps out the door, and I saw the bear just outside the stable window. With a mighty swipe of his paw he broke the glass. That was when I fired, aiming for the furry black chest.

The bear roared, then reared up into the air and fell back. I fired again and then again, and the bear lay quiet and still. The roar of the gun had been deafening to my ears, and now the silence seemed just as deafening.

Suddenly, I had an overpowering urge to make a dash for the house, away from this panic situation. I was nearly there when I saw the headlights of the approaching Jeep turning in the lane. Oh, what a relief! The men gathered excitedly around the big carcass. Kermit told me he was very proud of me. And I was embarrassed to find myself bursting into tears. I hope I never have to go through something like that again, but it's a good feeling to know the bear can't harm any of our stock now.

Part Two

Springtime at Tall Cedars

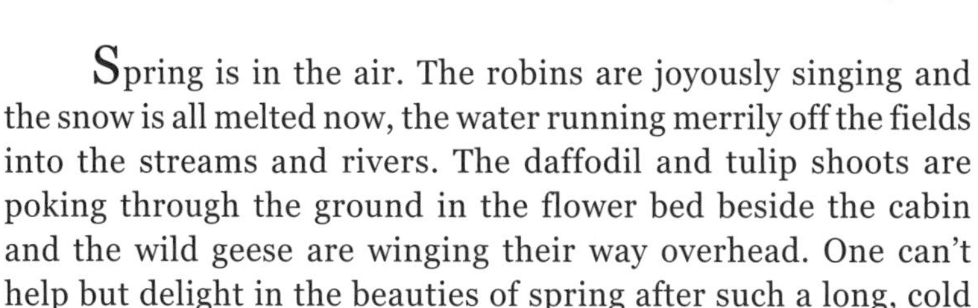

April 3

Spring is in the air. The robins are joyously singing and the snow is all melted now, the water running merrily off the fields into the streams and rivers. The daffodil and tulip shoots are poking through the ground in the flower bed beside the cabin and the wild geese are winging their way overhead. One can't help but delight in the beauties of spring after such a long, cold winter.

The calving season is well under way now, and so far it was a good season, though with the usual ups and downs. The vet had to come more than once and the frozen calf was the only one we lost. We lost one of our best cows, too. For awhile, we bottle-fed one calf, which Chuck kept in the laundry room of his bunkhouse beside an electric heater. It had lost its mother to mastitis, and we had a hard time teaching it to drink. Finally, it caught on and feeding it was a pleasure until we paired it up with a cow that had lost her calf. How rewarding it was to watch it nurse.

The big yellow school bus passes here every day, and today, as Kermit was hauling manure, it passed while Kermit was out near the road with his spreader. Two boys stuck their heads out the window and yelled some ungracious comments. Someone must have tattled on the boys, because a short time later a car drove up and waited at the end of the field until Kermit had finished his round.

A woman, with the two boys who had yelled at him, got out and said, "All right, boys, apologize." They both said they were sorry, and then she gave them a lecture on how manure fertilizes the crops, and she said if it weren't for the farmers, the world would soon be on a hunger strike. They seemed very quiet and subdued, and the woman very friendly. She asked if she could bring the boys out to tour the farm sometime to see all the animals and, of course, Kermit said she could.

Tonight Kermit brought in a big bouquet of blooming forsythia for me, knowing I like flowers. We put them in a jar, and they're a bright spot in our kitchen. He must be the most thoughtful and kindest husband ever. Tonight he helped me make peanut butter blossom cookies.

Peanut Butter Blossoms

1 egg, beaten
1/2 cup butter (soft)
1/2 teaspoon vanilla
3/4 cup brown sugar
1/2 cup white sugar
1/2 cup peanut butter
2 cups flour
1 teaspoon baking powder
1/4 teaspoon salt
2 cups peanut butter morsels

Preheat oven to 350°. In a bowl, mix the first six ingredients. Add the flour mixture, then stir in the peanut butter morsels. Drop by teaspoonful onto ungreased cookie sheets. Bake ten minutes. Makes six dozen two-inch cookies.

Thought for today: *The most beautiful things in the world cannot be seen or touched . . . they must be felt in the heart!*

April 4

I had a letter from Mom, and she had wonderful news! She will be here in a few days, along with Aunt Miriam and Uncle Nate, their daughter Sadie, and her friend Rosabeth. Since I had just cleaned the the house, I'll make another batch of filled doughnuts. Kermit is looking forward to visitors coming, too. It's easy to be happy in the spring when the soft breezes are blowing and the air is fragrant with the scent of early green things in the woods—and your loved ones are coming.

April 6

Our visitors arrived yesterday, sooner than I had expected them. What a delightful time—having heart-to-heart talks with Mom and visiting with Aunt Miriam and the girls. It was good that Kermit had Uncle Nate to visit with, or else he might have felt hen-pecked.

Mom gave me a lovely pink, blue, and white crib quilt she had made. She plans to give one to each of her children when they have their first baby and decided to bring it along, since she might not have a good chance to give it when I need it. I told her I hope I can use it soon.

Sadie, Rosabeth, and I explored the whole ranch together while the others took our horse and made calls with the church people in Swift River. We took Rindy along and kept a sharp lookout for the range bulls. No bears nor cougars have been seen in the vicinity lately, so we felt relatively safe from those. We found a patch of yellow marsh marigold near a swampy place, and went to tell Kermit, because those innocent-looking flowers are poisonous to cattle if they eat too many. It makes their stomachs swell and sometimes is even fatal if the vet isn't called soon enough.

We saw a doe and a wobbly fawn. The doe disappeared into the brush, and the fawn stared at us with its big luminous eyes for a few moments before it darted off after its mother, bleating a pathetic bleat. We had packed a picnic supper and ate out on the pine ridge, watching the sun disappear beneath the hills. The cows were out on the range now, with their frisky calves cavorting around them, the mothers contentedly munching the new green grass. The cliff swallows glided low and swooped up fast to catch the tiny bugs that appeared as soon as the warm weather came. They can be quite pesky to humans and cattle alike.

Kermit and Chuck, with Uncle Nate's help, were busy vaccinating calves, so we had this evening to ourselves, and we talked until late. I feel like I've only gotten to know Sadie and Rosabeth, and how I wish they could live just across the meadow from us. I'd love to run over to them every evening and share my day with them.

One by one the stars came out as the twilight sky grew dusky, and then the chorus in the hills began. The yipping and howling sounded like there were dozens of coyotes, but Kermit told me that they can throw their voices so that it's hard to tell just how many there are. Perhaps there are echoes from the opposite hills, too. The girls were delighted to hear them, saying it reminds them of the wild west in pioneer days.

On the way home, Rosabeth caught the gleam of two yellow eyes in the beam of her flashlight, and a wily coyote slunk away into the brush. Rindy wanted to follow it in the worst way, but we didn't allow her.

I believe I have a new appreciation for our ranch, seen through the eyes of Sadie and Rosabeth, and I realize I'm fortunate to live here even though it's isolated and lonely sometimes. They sure love it and said they'd like to come back in the wintertime to see the snow scenery. To think that I had been so tired of snow and so eager to see spring.

Back at the cabin, we sat on the porch steps and sang old-time songs the whole family used to sing together. Hearing them again brought an attack of *hemvey* (homesickness) and my eyes filled with tears. We sang, "In the Sweet By and By," "What a Friend we have in Jesus," "Life is Like a Mountain Railroad," "Where the Roses Never Fade," and "He Whispers Sweet Peace to Me."

We sang until Kermit joined us on the porch, and we sat and talked until the others drove in the lane, back from their visiting.

April 9 (Sunday)

Our visitors left two days ago already. Since they were here, I have such a longing to return home for a visit. Kermit has promised that as soon as he can afford it, I can go, and perhaps he will even be able to go also. I'm looking forward to it so much.

Today was a lovely warm day. After church services, Kermit and I decided to explore our neighborhood. About a half-mile down the road there is a path into the woods—a rutted woods road that must be quite secluded and shady in the summertime when the leaves are on the trees, but for now the most prominent thing in the woods are the big rocks. The path winds upward through the rocks, around and between them, until we're way up on top of the ridge and can see for miles around. There's not only one trail to the top, there are several different ways of reaching it. It must be a favorite place for campers and picnickers (according to the signs) for at one place we saw a little fireplace built of rock as well as several picnic tables. Other places had scenic picnic spots, too.

There are rivulets of running water here and there, cascading down over the rocks, and I suppose it all flows down into the same creek that crosses our meadow. From the top there are paths branching off in several directions. The side path we chose to follow led to a small dwelling built under a rocky hillside. It didn't seem like a very friendly place, for there were several chained dogs barking ferociously, so we turned around and took another path. The robins were singing and song sparrows trilling; we saw a bluebird high on a tree branch. When we rounded a curve in the path, we heard the sound of running water and followed it to where a tiny rivulet of rushing water cascaded down over a rock and into a little pool where bluebells, or grape hyacinths, were blooming all around it.

As we stood there admiring it, we heard the sound of hoofbeats coming down the path. Around the bend in the path, from behind a large rock, emerged a girl on a painted pony. She reined in her steed in surprise when she saw us and came to a quick halt.

"Hello," she said, a bit shyly. "Who are you?"

We introduced ourselves, telling her that we were the people who lived at Tall Cedars Homestead.

The girl's eyes lit up and she smiled when we told her that; she seemed glad to have us for neighbors. Her shyness evaporated fast and her friendly chattering soon had us at ease, too. She told us her name is Bethany Bryan, she is twelve years old, lives with her widowed mother just a half-mile back one of the woods roads that winds through that rocky woodside, which they call Rocky Ridge. She begged us to go home with her to meet her mother, assuring us that we would be more than welcome.

We followed Bethany and her pony until we came to a neat little bungalow, against a hillside but surrounded by a neat white picket fence. The place looked cheerful and well-kept, with window boxes at each window. I could imagine how lovely it would look in the summertime with colorful petunias cascading down over them. A pretty, middle-aged woman (Bethany's mother) came out on the porch and greeted us in a very friendly way, inviting us in for tea and cookies. It's good to know more of our neighbors.

I don't know about that other place in Rocky Ridge (where the chained dogs were barking), though, as Mrs. Bryan said they have never returned their overtures of friendship. The name of those people is Bentley, and they have teenage boys who tear around on their all-terrain vehicles, disturbing the peace of the neighborhood.

Bethany rode home with us—at least until the lane out of Rocky Ridge joined the road. On the way down, we discovered another little bubbling, laughing current of water that rippled over rocks, then disappeared under a culvert, with green-tinted grasses growing all around it. Bethany said that the woods are full of such places of running water in the spring, but later in the summer they nearly all dry up, until the next spring. It's a charming, enchanting place, and I'm happy to be living close to it. Kermit likes it, too, for he enjoys bird-watching, and I'm sure that both the birds and wildlife are abundant there in the woods. Next time we'll take binoculars.

Tonight a few friends dropped in to see our place, and now Kermit's out doing some necessary chores. I think I'll copy an inspiring verse.

> ***Golden Gem for today:*** *Blessed are those who hunger and thirst after righteousness, for they shall be filled. The secret of progress in the service of God is a strong yearning to live for Him.*

April 10

This must have been the day for visitors, for we've had several. A Mrs. Simmons, from the new house that was built south of here, stopped in this forenoon. She had her four-year-old daughter, Emily, along—a nice, quiet, and well-mannered little girl. Mrs. Simmons is looking for someone to watch Emily every day while she goes to her job as a teller at a bank. Since we were the closest farm, she decided to stop in and ask if I could do it or would know of someone who could.

I told her about our work here on the farm and she said that she's sure Emily wouldn't be a hindrance to me—she might even be a help. Emily likes to help do things like dusting furniture and drying dishes, plays quietly for long periods of time, and is satisfied with a sandwich at lunchtime—in short, is very little trouble. It sounded wonderful—Emily must be a very good little girl. After consulting with Kermit, I told Mrs. Simmons we would give it a try. It will keep me from getting lonely when Kermit is working out in the fields.

Emily has long, blonde hair cut in bangs in the front, merry dark eyes, and a wispy little smile. Her mother told her to give me a kiss before they left, and she obediently came over, hugged me, and kissed me on the cheek. Her first day here will be on Thursday, and I am looking forward to it.

Our other visitors were Mrs. Bryan and Bethany—a pleasant surprise! They walked over, and Bethany carried a gift—a beautifully frosted chocolate cake. They seemed like old friends before the evening was over. Mrs. Bryan wears lipstick and has her hair cut, but she did wear a dress and seems to have a pleasant personality. Bethany wanted to see all our animals and asked if she could come over sometimes to help me with whatever I'm doing. I told her I'd be happy to have her come.

Ya well, it's time to mix meat loaf for supper if I want it to be ready when Kermit comes in. Scalloped corn would be good with that and mashed potatoes and a salad.

> **Golden Gem for today:** *It was in His great love that the Father gave the Son. It was out of love that Jesus gave Himself. The taking, the having of Jesus is the entrance to a life in the love of God; this is the highest life. Through faith we must press into love and dwell there.*

April 11

Snow! Every bush and tree twig is covered with it, but it's not deep. We hitched up Patsy and drove down to see the Mullets. They are like family to Kermit, so we had a very enjoyable day. They gave us a good dinner, and visiting them was almost as good as it would be to be able to visit my parents.

Mrs. Mullet (Mom) wondered if I could use a helper when school is out in May, since she has a whole row of daughters and not enough work for them all at home. Of course, I jumped at the chance, so we're planning on getting twelve-year-old Treva.

If things keep on going the way they are now, we should soon have a houseful. Kermit has lined up a young *Gnecht* (hired boy) for the summer, too. His name is Jared Miller, a first cousin to Treva Mullet. They go to the same school and know each other quite well. Jared is a year older, but they're in the same grade. They, along with Emily, should keep things lively around here. It will mean more time spent in cooking, canning, and doing laundry, but it will be worth it. There's a lot of acreage to this farm, and Kermit will be really busy.

April 12

Spring is here again after our onion snow yesterday, with warm breezes blowing, turtle doves cooing, song sparrows singing, "Maid, maid, put on your teakettle," and robins sweetly trilling. Several times during the night I thought I heard a soft nickering sound outside—like a horse's questioning whinny—but I was too sleepy to investigate. Finally, it woke me, and I told Kermit; together we went outside.

It was four o'clock in the morning, and the stars were twinkling in the velvety sky; the waning moon cast a faint glow over the fields, trees, and hills of the surrounding farm. As we searched the place, I realized that it now seems like "home sweet home" to us. I'm afraid it will be hard for us to leave these dear, familiar scenes someday, as attached to them as we already are.

There was no sign of a horse anywhere and I was beginning to think I must have been imagining things. Then we walked out to the road and, sure enough, there trotting along outside the meadow fence came our Patsy, whinnying softly and seemingly glad to see us. Kermit caught her by the halter and led her back to the barn.

It was then that an old rattle-trap of a car came chugging down the road and slowing down at our place. The window was lowered and a guy rudely yelled something out at us, then went on his way. Kermit thought it very likely was someone who lives in the house we saw in Rocky Ridge (the Bentleys), and who Bethany Bryan was telling us about. Wonder what he was doing at this hour. It doesn't sound like we can expect much neighborliness from him.

Patsy's gate was open. She must be adept at opening gates, so we must take extra precautions after this. It makes me shudder to think of what could have happened had that car hit Patsy.

April 13

Emily's first day here, and I think she's exactly as her mother described her. She wanted to explore the barn to see what animals we have and then begged to climb the ladder that leads to the hay mow to see what is up there. I followed closely behind her to make sure she didn't fall. Up in the mow we heard soft, mewing sounds and in a corner behind a hay bale found a nest of five little kittens—three of them gray and white, one three-colored, and one yellow. Emily was absolutely enchanted and would have liked to stay there all day playing with them, but the worried mama cat came on the scene and I persuaded Emily that it was time for us to leave. Back in the house we put the finishing touches to the meal I was preparing.

Emily helped me make potato rolls (she loved to help punch the dough). This afternoon after she had had her nap and the buns were baked and cooled, we took a snack of potato rolls, raspberry jelly, and chocolate milk out the field to Kermit where he was plowing. It's good to breathe in the wholesome odor of freshly plowed soil in the spring sunshine. Dick and Daisy needed a rest anyway. Emily begged to be allowed to "ride a horse," so Kermit set her up on Daisy's broad back for a few minutes. She loved it and wasn't in the least bit scared.

On the way back Emily picked a bouquet of dandelions for her mother. But when her mother came to get her, she wasn't ready to leave and hid under the table, pulling the tablecloth down so her mother wouldn't see her. But her mother pulled her out; Emily was giggling and then was glad to see her mother after all. She's a sweet little girl and I don't think we'll be sorry we consented to babysit her.

The potato roll recipe was from Delphine (who is a very good cook) and it turned out real well, so I'll copy it here:

Potato Rolls

6 potatoes, cooked (save water)
1 cup butter
1 cup sugar
2 eggs
1 teaspoon salt

2 tablespoons yeast, dissolved in 1 cup warm potato water
7 cups Occident flour, sifted

Mash potatoes. Add butter, sugar, eggs, salt, and yeast and water mixture. Slowly add flour. Knead for 10 minutes and let rise until double in bulk. Knead down. Divide dough into 4 pieces. Divide each piece into 8 small rolls and arrange on cookie sheets. Let rise until double. Bake at 350° for about 25 minutes.

April 14

Springtime must be the loveliest time of year! There are several beds of blooming tulips, daffodils, and hyacinths under the trees in the front yard. The red Emperor tulips are blooming, and soon the yellow, lavender, white, and candy-striped will be open. There is one round bed of tulips under a cedar tree that is all red and white tulips (red and white Emperor) and that has a very striking and lovely effect. Emily loves to pick bouquets, and soon there will be enough out there that it won't matter. We have two bouquets in vases now and they brighten up our kitchen for as long as they last.

After the chores were done, Kermit got out the work horses, Dick and Daisy, and plowed and harrowed the garden, all ready for planting. What fun it was, digging in the soft, warm earth, planting peas, potatoes, lettuce, cabbage, parsley, spinach, onions, red beets, and radishes, while a robin sang sweetly from the spruce tree. We weren't quite done when a soft, gentle spring rain came slowly and steadily, sinking into the thirsty ground.

We finished in the rain and were chilly when we came in. We found that the fire was out in the Gem-Pak, so Kermit rebuilt the fire and I made popcorn. We had a cozy evening with the rain falling outside. "Time doth softly, sweetly glide, when there's love at home."

Golden Gem for today: *It is only the love of God coming in that will cast out self. When God brings a man to see all that there is in Christ, and to receive Christ fully, the power of Christ's death can come upon him and he can die to sin, and if he dies to sin, he dies to self.*

April 16 (Sunday)

Kermit and I decided to pack a picnic lunch and to explore some of the surrounding woods and hills. The woodlands and pine groves are so vast that I don't think we've seen them all yet.

The great, beautiful world around us on such a lovely day in spring seemed breathtakingly beautiful. The chorus of birdsong, the pretty wildflowers, the lush green grasses, the majestic pines, and the blue, blue sky—it was all so unbearably awesome. And yet, it wasn't all beautiful.

While hiking to the top of a ridge, we surprised a coyote feasting on the carcass of a dead deer. It quickly slunk away and we were about to do the same when we heard a mewing sound from a thicket of climbing honeysuckle.

"It's a kitten!" I cried. "Let's rescue it." But it wasn't—it was a catbird. We also saw and heard bluebirds, wood pee-wees, pine siskins, and other birds I couldn't identify. We also saw a lot of wildlife, for it is plentiful in the woods.

Tonight after the chores were done we sat on the front steps and watched the moon rising over the pine hills and listened to the whippoorwills calling. The yipping and howling of the coyotes no longer frighten me; it's all the sounds of home to me now. I think I'm putting down roots here at last—it's home, sweet home. Kermit said that to him, it was love at first sight. We have so much to be thankful for.

We took another long walk up in Rocky Ridge and discovered another place we hadn't seen before, although we were sure no one lives there. We took a trail we hadn't taken before and came to an old tumbledown, abandoned house. The doors were hanging crookedly on their hinges, some of the window panes were broken or missing, and the shutters were swaying in the breeze. Outside there was a grassy, weed-overgrown cobblestone walk leading to the broken-down front porch, and there were a few weather-beaten evergreen bushes and scraggly flowering shrubs which were all that remained of the landscaping.

If that old house could talk, it could probably tell a lot of stories of bygone days. We stopped by the little waterfall, which has dwindled into a trickle, but the little rock-lined pool is still overflowing and will stay that way as long as its water source is not completely cut off. We sat and reminisced undisturbed. There were other hikers and picnickers in the woods, but none close by.

April 17

Last night I woke about midnight and went to the window to close it. I thought I saw a movement in the lane near the barn, so I stood watching for a few minutes, and there really was something there. I told Kermit and he joined me at the window. We saw the outline of a pickup truck with no lights on, inching its way past the barn.

Kermit quickly dressed and hurried quietly out, keeping in the shadows of the shrubbery. There's a gas pump behind the barn, and he figured that's where the pickup was going. He knew that the tank was empty, but he wanted to see if that was really what the prowlers were after.

Sure enough, when he crept up behind the garage, Kermit saw two boys trying to pump gas. He decided to give them a scare. Taking a blade of grass between his thumbs, he whistled through it. When that shrill whistle broke the stillness of the night, the boys wasted no time getting back into the truck and tearing out the lane at full speed, probably taking the curve out to the road on two wheels, the way it sounded. They roared up the road—the sound echoing back from the hills. I don't think they'll be back again soon.

A funny thing happened today—I had washed and waxed the kitchen floor this forenoon, so when Kermit came in for dinner, he left his shoes on the porch so he wouldn't track dirt in. After dinner when he wanted to put his shoes back on, they were nowhere to be found.

Emily was innocent, for she hadn't gone outside the whole time Kermit was there. She helped to hunt for the shoes, too, and was the one who found them, under a juniper bush in the backyard. She also found the culprit that had taken them—a furry brown stray dog. He came out from under the bush, wagging his tail in a very friendly way. He was probably just a pup, but already pretty big. Emily was delighted, and in no time at all they were great friends. She named him Snickers. He probably belongs to one of the neighbors, who will quite likely come looking for him soon. He has made friends with Rindy already.

> **Golden Gem for today:** *Jesus said to Peter, "Deny thyself;" and again, "Thou wilt deny Me." There is no choice for us, we must either deny self or deny Christ. Absolute surrender? How am I to live that life? The Father points to the beloved Son and says, "This is My beloved Son in whom I am well pleased." Hear Him, follow Him, live like Him, let Christ be the rule of your life.*

April 18

Bethany Bryan came over on her pony tonight and stayed awhile. I told her she can watch while I *shore* (spade) my flower beds, so she joined me out in the yard. While I worked, she chatted away, telling me all about her school life. The youngest Bentley boy—Joey, aged thirteen—is in her grade at school and is a troublemaker. There are a few Amish children from another district going to that school (because there's no parochial school close), and Joey picks on them, especially Elma, the girl who sits at the desk in front of him. According to Bethany, the teacher, Mrs. Helm, chooses to ignore what's going on and even seems to turn her back on what the boy does, which isn't right.

I asked Bethany what sort of things Joey does, and she says he does whatever he can to get Elma into trouble. He writes notes (copying her handwriting) and puts them at places where he's sure the teacher will find them and then says he saw Elma passing them. The teacher must know he's lying, but she always takes his side. He jabs Elma with his pencil and pulls her *Kapp* out of place. On the playground he trips her, sticks out his tongue, and mocks her and her younger brother and sister. Oh, well, it probably won't be long until they transfer to the nearest parochial school, even though there isn't one close.

Bethany also told me about her dad, whom she does not remember because she was just a baby when he died. He had stopped on the road to help an elderly lady who had a flat tire, and while he was changing the tire, another vehicle hit him and he was killed. It's a good way to remember him—the thought that he was doing a kind deed for someone else.

Bethany stayed until it was nearly dark, and we've become very good friends. She said she hopes to find a husband someday who's as nice as Kermit, and I told her that would be hard to do.

> **Golden Gem for today:** *As each seed bears fruit after its kind, and of its very own nature, and the fruit in its turn again bears a seed, so the Spirit of Christ was the hidden seed-life of which the cross was the fruit. And the cross again became the seed of which the Spirit is the fruit.*

April 19

Kermit made a rose arbor for me today and painted it white. He had given me a rose bush for my birthday, and he knew I wanted an arbor, too, and now it is finished. How kind of him!

Emily is becoming quite attached to us and life here on the farm. Often when her mother comes to pick her up, she's not ready to go. She and Snickers, the pup, are inseparable, too, and we're hoping that no one will claim him.

Emily begs to have a dress like mine, and her mother gave me permission to make her one sometime. She wanted a *Kapp*, too, but I told her she'll have to wait until she's older (by that time I know she won't be interested anymore). She's learning Dutch words, too. She calls her doll *Bupp*, our kittens, *bustein*, and the mother cat, *katz*. The horse is a *gaul*, the cow is *kew*, and the chickens are *hinkle*. The table is "the dish," and the rocking chair *shuckle shtule*. She is such a very loveable and interesting little girl; I long all the more to have one of my own. Or a little boy just like Kermit. Sweet dreams . . .

April 20

We're having very summer-like weather, and the garden things are growing nicely. Some of the fruit trees around here are starting to blossom, and soon it will be the battle with the

weeds and grass again! I spent the afternoon working in the garden. I planted several rows of string beans and then a long row of pink and white petunias along the border. Let's hope we won't have a killing frost now! I also planted several rows of sweet corn and will plant a bigger batch later; that way, all our corn-on-the-cob won't be ready at once. Emily helped drop in the seeds, and Snickers wanted to help, too, sending the dirt flying, until we finally penned him in the woodshed until we were done.

The leaves are coming out on the big maple tree in the backyard, and the robins are busy building a nest in it. I longed to go barefoot since the soil in the garden was warm, but I didn't, because I knew Emily would want to also, and her mother hadn't given her permission.

We washed the carriage next, and Emily was up on top if it, scrubbing away, when her mother drove in. I was half afraid she wouldn't like it, but she just laughed and said Emily was having the time of her life. Emily threw a little fit because she had to leave just then, but when her mother told her they would stop at the store for candy and that she could watch TV until Daddy came home, she finally gave up and went along willingly. I wonder what would have happened had she not given up and simply refused to go.

Oh, I see that Kermit has Patsy hitched to the two-wheeled cart and is ready to go for a drive, so I'll finish this later.

April 23 (Sunday)

Today was a good day for going on a walk after church services. Walking up the trails in Rocky Ridge, we saw that some of the trees and bushes are beginning to flower already, and the noisy, gurgling little rivulets of water are still going strong. We had the binoculars along this time, and Kermit was able to identify a lot of birds. We sat on a big rock, just relaxing and enjoying the beauty of our surroundings. Soon our lovely peace was disturbed by a four-wheeler that came tearing down the trail. One of the Bentley boys roared past and seemed to purposely rev up his engine extra noisily just as he passed us.

He apparently chugged up another trail, on up to Lookout Point, the highest spot in Rocky Ridge, where there is a view for miles. We saw him and two others up there, and next thing we knew, stones and even rocks came raining down through the trees, a fair warning for us to leave, we supposed. And leave we did—as fast as we could.

On the way down we met Bethany on her pony, and she was quite indignant when we told her about the boys. She said that the Bentleys don't own an inch of Rocky Ridge besides the half-acre their home is on. The scenic land is owned by a gentleman who lives in the city and has made the public welcome on his property—picnickers, hikers, and birdwatchers. Bethany threatened to call the police, but we persuaded her not to since the boys hadn't really tried to hit us, and it might just make things worse.

In the evening we hitched Patsy to the carriage and drove close to the Five-Star Ranch, where there is a scenic lake, and Kermit and I went for a boat ride—just the two of us. It was so peaceful with the birds twittering softly from the treetops as the dusky twilight descended. The mellow sounds and breezes of springtime were all around us. The fragrance of the moist earth where growing things were pushing through and the peacefully flowing water with a few wild ducks landing on it and swimming quickly out of sight was relaxing. We sat there together until late, enjoying the beauty and peace of our surroundings (without fear of a disturbance from the Bentley boys) and then tied the boat and headed for home.

> ***Bible verse for today:*** *For, lo, the winter is past, the rain is over and gone; the flowers appear on the earth; the time of the singing of birds is come, and the voice of the turtle is heard in our land. (Song of Solomon 2:11, 12)*

May 1

We had a visitor today, a lady by the name of Mrs. Elegant (at least, that's what it sounded like). She said she lives several miles upcountry and was driving around and decided to stop in.

She came in carrying a cage containing a small, dark, furry animal—a pet ferret whose name is Mini. I felt a bit repulsed at first, feeling sure that it must be a not-too-distant relative of a rat, but Emily was simply enchanted. She asked to be allowed to hold Mini, and Mrs. Elegant (as we call her) took her out of the cage and handed her to Emily.

They took to each other immediately. The ferret scampered up Emily's arm and planted an inquisitive "kiss" on her cheek, and Emily was hooked! They romped about on the lawn, chasing each other playfully, the ferret scampering here and there so quickly and playfully until Emily collapsed with peals of laughter.

Mrs. Elegant said, "I'm looking for a new home for Mini. Would you be willing to take her? Ferrets make wonderfully playful pets and companions, and I'd give you this cage and a bag of feed. I'm going to be moving into a condominium soon, and pets won't be allowed." She scooped up Mini and caressed her lovingly while tears coursed down her cheeks, saying, "It won't be easy for me to give her up," dabbing at her cheeks all the while.

Emily was jumping up and down excitedly, asking, "May we keep her, Joy? May we? Please say yes!"

I told her to go ask Kermit, and she was off in a flash, running for the barn. She returned pulling Kermit along by the hand. I think Kermit's opinion of the ferret was the same as mine—too much like a rat, and we have enough of those pests in the barn at times!

But Emily's pleas won him over and we reluctantly gave our consent, intending to send the ferret home with Emily's mom, if possible. But when Mrs. Simmons saw the little creature, she threw up her hands in horror! No way would she allow a rodent in her house. And so we've gotten ourselves a new pet, which is a great responsibility, because Mrs. Elegant will surely want to come back to see Mini every now and then. If Mini is not well cared for, it will break her heart. But at least Emily is very happy, and if all goes well, they will be a big pastime for each other.

Tonight Kermit and I walked back to the little garden we had planted a few weeks ago. The things are up nicely and a robin sang so joyously from the wild raspberry thicket down by the fence. I just longed to see the old orchard back home in full bloom—the trees laden with white and pink blossoms—and the big lilac bush covered with sweet-scented lavender blossoms. Most of all, I longed to see Mom and Pop and the rest of the family, and dear ones back home. I can't believe now that I was restless and discontent there, for I have such a longing to go back, if only just for a visit. It must be human nature, always wanting what is not.

I made another page for my inspirational calendar when we got in, and the verse I copied on it was, "I have learned in whatsoever state I am therewith to be content." On the back, I copied, "Godliness with contentment is great gain."

Golden Gem for today: *How often we trouble about things and about praying for them, instead of going back to the root of things and saying, "Lord, I only crave to be the receptacle of what the will of God means for me; of the power and the gift and the love and the Spirit of God."*

May 11 (Ascension Day)

We had a "family" gathering today here at Tall Cedars Homestead, or rather, all that we consider family (Kermit's adopted family, the Mullets). It was the first big company meal I made alone, and although I was a bit flustered by the time the guests began to arrive, I felt like I had everything under control. Maybe I shouldn't have written "alone," for Kermit helped by stretching the table to its full length and putting in all the leaves, and he helped to set the table. He brought the cans of peaches up from the cellar and even sliced the homemade bread.

Emily was here, too, for her mother went to her job just like any other day (the English don't celebrate the Ascension of Christ in any way, I guess). Her job was to entertain Mini and keep her off the table. I would greatly have preferred to keep the ferret locked in her cage, but Emily wouldn't hear of it. That would be too cruel. She sat shyly on the big rocker, holding Mini while the guests arrived.

Dad Mullet's eyes got big when he saw Mini, for he had never seen a ferret before. He sat down beside Emily, and they soon had an animated conversation going, with Emily telling him all about her pet. We womenfolk mashed the potatoes, sliced the baked ham, browned the butter for the noodles and peas, and mixed the salad.

I told Emily to put Mini in her cage while we ate dinner, but apparently she didn't obey, for when we were all seated at the table and had our heads bowed to say grace, we heard a rattling sound. There was Mini, up on the table digging around in the candy dish for her favorite kind! It was rather amusing to us because we've gotten used to her, but I'm afraid to some of the others (especially Mom Mullet), it was too much like seeing a rat on the table.

Emily was dispatched straightaway to pen up the ferret, and this time I made sure she did so. But after dinner, she smuggled Mini out of her cage again, then apparently forgot about her when she ran off to play with the children. Grandpa went to take his usual short after-dinner nap on the bed in the *Commar* (downstairs bedroom), and as he always does, he put his gold tooth on the nightstand beside the bed (so he won't swallow it). When he woke up, he reached for his tooth and it wasn't there.

We searched all over for the gold tooth, never once thinking that the ferret might have been the culprit. When Emily came in-

side, her first thought was to find Mini, and there she was, asleep on the cushion in the doll bed, the gold tooth clutched in her little "hands."

Mrs. Elegant stopped in tonight to see her little Mini again (not realizing we were celebrating Ascension Day), and when we told her what Mini had done, she laughed. She said that is typical of a "ferret" which in Latin means "little thief."

All in all, we had a very good day; the meal turned out okay, and we had a good time visiting with the family. I hope we didn't forget the real meaning of the day.

May 17

Our *Maad* and *Gnecht* arrived! Treva is a bouncy, outgoing girl with red hair and green eyes. I don't think she has a shy bone in her body, which may, or may not, be an asset. (I think she'll be a good one to wait on hay customers.) Her cousin Jared is freckle-faced with a wave of sandy-colored hair tumbling over his forehead. A frequent shake of his head keeps the hair out of his eyes. His personality seems to be similar to Treva's, and they seem more like brother and sister tha cousins. Kermit said they could be rather a handful together, with neither of them having a meek or quiet personality. Ya, well, they're bound to keep things lively around here, and hopefully the work will fly.

Emily tags after Treva constantly, chattering away, with Mini perched on her. If they are outside, Snickers the pup is with them, too. Emily didn't take her usual nap because she didn't want to miss a thing with Treva.

This evening, Wynn and Jill (Delphine and Art's granddaughter) paid us a visit. They are getting married in June and asked me to make a wall hanging for their living room wall. It took awhile to decide what pattern they wanted. We talked about their upcoming marriage, discussing how their ceremony differs from our weddings.

Jill said she would never promise to love, honor, and obey her husband. The first two, yes; but not obey. She asked if I had promised to obey Kermit, and I told her that word isn't in the question that is asked during the wedding ceremony, but a word that means "to be in subjection to" which means "under the authority of." She thought that didn't sound too bad, and neither do I.

The way it appears now, Wynn and Jill won't have any financial difficulties, since it seems they have plenty of money.

May 21 (Sunday)

Our peonies along the porch are blooming, and we all spend as much time as possible out on the porch, for the blooms are simply gorgeous. They are prettier than a picture, for they're **real** and fragrant! Emily loves to gather bouquets for the kitchen and for her mother, who goes into raptures of ecstasy (real or pretended) over them.

Last evening after our *Maad* and *Gnecht* had gone home for Sunday, Kermit and I headed for Rocky Ridge, eager to try out the new night vision gadget that Kermit had ordered through the mail. It's similar to binoculars but is designed only for use at night. When we look through it in the darkness, we can see objects clearly, almost as well as in daylight. I don't understand how it works, but it does.

We waited until dark, then headed for the ridge. We hoped we wouldn't be seen by any of the Bentleys as we hiked up the trail close to the old abandoned house, where the woods were dense. Apparently we weren't seen (perhaps Bentleys were away), for we neither saw nor heard anything of them. We figured that if any of them came by in their four-wheelers, we'd have plenty of time to hide in the brush before they would see us.

Near the old house we found a suitable flat rock next to a watering place, where we spread out our blanket and lay in wait to see what wildlife we could see. A great-horned owl was hooting eerily from somewhere in the treetops, and the wavering call of a screech owl from somewhere up in the Ridge reverberated through the treetops. Frogs croaked, and in the thickets we could hear the rustlings and stirrings of small creatures. Night insects chorused all around us.

When it was my turn for the gadget, I scanned the surrounding thickets for wildlife and was rewarded with seeing two rabbits going by, hippity-hop, not ten feet away, unaware of our presence. Then, as soon as they were out of my range of vision, a mother skunk ambled by, followed by four tiny baby skunks. They were so cute, and their antics laughable as they stalked insects and pounced on dried leaves. I handed the gadget to Kermit and he watched until they were out of sight.

A few minutes later, he handed it back noiselessly, but I just knew he had seen something exciting. It was a masked mother raccoon with two little kits, stopping at the water hole. The mother began to feel around the bottom of the pool with her "hands," and came up with a minnow, which she tossed to the kits. One quickly pounced on it, and his sibling did the same, trying to snatch it from him. But in a second, another minnow was tossed to them, and they were both happy. They swished their prize around in the water before they began to eat it. I was so fascinated that I almost forgot to give Kermit a turn. It was a good thing that the breeze was in our faces, or else they would have caught our scent.

After that, we had a long wait until an opossum stalked into view. We took turns watching in breathless excitement when we discovered that all along her tail hung tiny baby opossums. Then for a long time there was nothing but the stirrings of mice in the thickets. Suddenly, we were rewarded with a sight that was well worth the wait.

A red fox came into view and jumped up onto a rock off to the side of the trail, about twenty feet away. His back was turned to us and he was sniffing the breeze with his head cocked to the side, his regal white-tipped tail streaming out behind him. After awhile, he flattened himself down on the rock, then leapt forward and pounced on something in the thickets. He trotted off with his catch (probably a mouse), and that was all we saw of him.

We thought it was a well-spent evening, but if we would have known what was going on at home, we would have quickly changed our minds. I'll write about that next time, for I see that Kermit has Dick hitched to the harrow, all ready to cultivate the garden, and I must go lead the horse for him.

May 25

Now I'll write about what happened here Saturday evening while we were out watching the wildlife in Rocky Ridge. It sure is nothing at all pleasant to think about, but what's done is done. When we came back to the kitchen and Kermit lit the gas lantern, the clock said 11:30. We were about to head for bed, when Kermit asked if I was sure I had locked the front door, for Art Rivers had told him there were burglars on a rampage in our neighborhood. I thought I had, but he decided to double check it.

The floor was littered with broken glass! A window had been knocked in, and the stack of quilts and wall hangings that Treva's mother had sent over was gone! They had been here so I could choose a pattern for the wall hanging for Jill and Wynn, and were under our responsibility for safekeeping, and now they were gone. What a feeling of dismay! Oh, what would Treva's mother say?

Kermit said that whoever it was had probably seen us leave the house and knew no one was home. Who could it have been? The Bentley boys? But we can't blame them unless we have proof. We reported it to the police on Monday morning and they came out to investigate but as yet have no clues. Kermit replaced the broken window, and it was a good thing he did it right away, for tonight we had a heavy thunderstorm with a lashing, driven rain that would have soaked the room in a few minutes.

> **Golden Gem for today:** *Not only what is given up to Christ received back again to become doubly our own, but the forsaking all is followed by receiving all. We abide in Christ more fully as we forsake all to follow Him. As we count all things lost for His sake, we are found in Him.*

May 26

We are in the midst of strawberry season, and Treva and Emily have been going to the neighbors' every morning to pick some. We have enough canned, but Treva enjoys picking and she gets paid for it. Jared goes, too, whenever Kermit can spare him, but he's not as fond of it as Treva. Emily helps, too—she carefully picks a handful and eats them daintily and slowly, savoring every bite.

Bethany came over tonight and got acquainted with both Treva and Jared. They were busy hoeing in the sweet corn patch, and Bethany wanted to help. We didn't have another hoe, so she pulled weeds in the rows. When I took out a pitcher full of iced mint tea, they were chatting away like old friends. Bethany invited them both over tomorrow evening to try out a new game of hers. Jared said he won't go if he is the only boy, but she begged nicely and said the game was table hockey, and they were having ice cream cones.

At last, Jared said he would go if Bethany would let him ride her pony. I think he just wanted to pretend he didn't want to go and wanted to be begged. He's bringing his own pony and cart over next week, then he and Treva can drive back and forth by themselves. Mrs. Bryan will take them home tomorrow evening after their visit.

Kermit mowed hay this afternoon, and now, at twilight, the air is fragrant with the wonderful scent of new-mown hay. The rose bush he gave me has a few big, lovely pink roses on it, and with the background of the white lattice rose arbor, it is a beautiful picture. It's full moon tonight, and a screech owl is calling from the fence row trees. I heard a fox barking from the direction of Rocky Ridge; perhaps it was the one we saw. Kermit's coming in with the horses now and singing "*Das Lob Lied*," the praise song.

Thought for today: *Love that is shared*
Is a beautiful thing
It enriches the soul
And makes the heart sing.

May 27

Today was a day in which everything seemed to go wrong! I wonder if other people have such days, too. Mrs. Elegant stopped in tonight, and when I told her about our misfortunes, she said that Murphy's Law must be in effect (whatever that meant). I didn't like to show my ignorance by asking.

First, when we got to the barn this morning, there was a leak in a water pipe and the cattle pen was flooded. That made us a lot of extra work, and breakfast was late. I had put a breakfast casserole into the oven of the gas stove before I went out to help with the chores (Treva and Jared had left early for an hour of berry picking before breakfast), and by the time I got back to the kitchen, the smell of burnt casserole greeted me (I bemoan my forgetfulness). It was browned to a crisp, and not a particle of it was edible.

Kermit ate breakfast (cold cereal) in a great hurry, saying the hay was fit for baling and he wanted to get it done before the rain came. But before he even got the horses hitched, rain began to pour and continued all forenoon. The hay was ruined in a short time—good for nothing except maybe mulching. So Kermit decided that while it was raining might be a good time to go to town and get some necessary shopping done. But when he led Patsy from the barn to hitch to the carriage, the horse walked with an unmistakable limp. We thought some mysterious ailment must have afflicted her overnight, until we saw that Dick was loose and must have kicked Patsy. The big lummox!

In the afternoon, Mom Mullet came driving in the lane with their horse hitched to the trotting buggy and asked if I want to go along to the store. *At last,* I thought, *one bright spot in this dismal day!* I quickly went for my shoes and bonnet, donned a clean apron, and hopped up beside Mom on the buggy. (Treva and Jared were helping Kermit clean out the old woodshed.)

We were in good spirits, all ready to catch up on the latest news, but we hadn't gone a half-mile before it began to rain again.

Oh, no! Shall we turn around? But Mom decided that getting a bit wet wouldn't hurt us and I agreed, so we went on. Just around the next turn came Emanuel B. and his wife on their spring wagon, holding a big black umbrella above their heads. This was too much for Mom's horse (who was new to these country roads) and he bolted, leaping up over the roadside bank. The buggy lurched precariously, on the verge of overturning, and there was a sharp crack. When it was all over, the buggy was still on its wheels, but the shafts were broken.

Emanuel kindly came to our aid while his wife watched their horse. He unhitched Mom's horse and surveyed the damage. He said he was very sorry (very apologetically), and that had he known our horse would be scared, he would have folded up the umbrella. We assured him that it wasn't his fault. We led the horse back to our farm and I pulled the buggy there; it was slightly downhill, or I wouldn't have been able to.

Our plans of shopping were ruined, because the broken shaft had scraped the horse's leg and it was bleeding a bit. Fortunately, Mrs. Bryan drove in just then and, seeing our predicament, offered to drive Mom Mullet home.

After supper and the chores were done and the children had gone, Kermit and I decided to go to bed early because it was raining again. I was thinking it was a relief that this day was nearly over, when a car came in the lane. It was one of our hay customers; he had bought some hay awhile back and said it was not of good quality and was unsatisfactory (even though he had examined it before he bought it). So we gave back his money and decided to be thankful that it was nothing worse. I thought of the verse:

It's easy enough to be pleasant
When life flows along like a song,
But the man worthwhile
Is the man who will smile
When everything seems to go wrong.

May 28 (Sunday)

Another beautiful Sunday nearly gone. We attended services in a neighboring district, then stopped in at Rachel and Ben's (a married couple just our age and good friends of ours) on the way back. We told them we just planned to rest the horses for a few minutes (it was a warm day), but they would hear nothing of it. Ben unhitched our horse, fed and watered him, and Rachel said that supper would be ready in a jiffy, and that we are staying, with no ifs, ands, or buts allowed (smiles).

Kermit helped Ben with the evening chores, and Rachel took me upstairs to show me her little nursery—the room adjoining their bedroom. She had papered the walls with Rock-a-bye Baby wallpaper, and there is a dressing table, a little white bassinet with lacy frills all around it, and a diaper stacker already hanging on the wall—ready for the little newcomer who is due to arrive in late August. I couldn't help but feel a pang of envy and an empty feeling inside. How I wish these joys of anticipation were mine. But I want to be patient and not let my life be marred with discontent.

After supper we sat and visited until the stars came out and the fireflies dotted the lawn. Their farm isn't as well-kept as some are, but they have done a lot of work on it and it's looking a lot better than it did when they moved there. There's a long row of blooming geraniums along their garden, and the old board fence along the lane has recently received a fresh coat of white paint. Kermit said it wouldn't *forlate* him with a farm like that if he could be the owner, even though there's still room for a lot of improvements.

It's bedtime now, but Kermit has gone to check on the cattle, so I'll copy a Golden Gem:

> ***Golden Gem for today:*** *Intercession is the most perfect form of prayer; it is the prayer Christ ever liveth to pray on His throne. As love of our profession and work sink away in the tender compassion of Christ, that love will compel us to prayer.*

May 30

What a surprise we had this morning when Treva's parents brought her over for the week. They were followed by Mrs. Bryan and Bethany in their car. Treva was a bundle of excitement when she came to the door, and so was Jared when he arrived a few minutes later (he drove down with his own pony and cart this time). We could hardly believe it at first, but it's true—all our stolen quilts and wall hangings have been found! A police car drove in a few minutes later with them, and now they're safely back here and not harmed in any way. What a relief!

The story of their rescue began on Saturday evening, although we didn't know about it then. Bethany had invited Treva and Jared over to play her new game, so they walked over, and Mrs. Bryan had offered to take them home afterward. This is the story they gave to me: They played table hockey for awhile, and then when they had tired of that, they decided to go exploring in Rocky Ridge. Jared rode Bethany's pony, as she had promised he could. From Lookout Point, they saw the Bentley family leave, so they had the woods to themselves, except for a few hikers.

Bethany came up with the grand idea of exploring the old abandoned house (or haunted house, as they call it). They entered by way of the sagging front door and found that the floor boards of the old kitchen were in very poor shape. They could see down into the cellar where there was a spring of water flowing out of a pipe into a big trough and on out through an old iron grate opening into a little stream outside.

Someone had put a few solid planks across the crumbling floorboards to a not-so-old-looking ladder near the far wall. The ladder led to an open trap door to the second floor. There were no stairs. This aroused Jared's curiosity, and he headed for the ladder, daring the girls to follow. Not wanting to appear cowardly, they bravely followed.

Upstairs, things were in better shape. The floor boards were still solid, probably because they were above the dampness. The floor had been swept, although some cobwebs hung from the ceiling. There was an old table in the center of the room, and a few chairs. Against one wall stood an antique chest, still in good shape. Jared tried to open the lid, but it was locked. This made them curious and they decided to hunt for a key. Treva found it up on a ledge near the sloping roof.

Jared unlocked the chest and found quilts and wall hangings in big black garbage bags. Right away they suspected they were our stolen stuff, but weren't sure. They decided to re-lock the chest and put the key back where it was, then go home and tell their parents. On the way back to Bethany's house they got the brilliant notion of trying to solve the mystery themselves—to be amateur detectives. They suspected the Bentley boys, but would have to have proof. They could hide in the woods and keep watch over the haunted house, and if they saw the Bentleys going in there, they would know. Then they would quickly call the police.

But their idea wasn't very practical, because the next day was Sunday; besides, how or when would they do the spying? On Sunday afternoon Jared's family was at Treva's house, and together they decided they had better tell their parents. The police were called yesterday morning. The quilts were retrieved and Treva's mother identified them, and now we have our quilts back.

The police are investigating the case. We're fairly certain it was the Bentley boys because they could have seen us leave our house, but the police need proof. They'll question the boys and follow every possible clue. It's a good feeling to have the quilts back! I think those boys probably had no idea how to go about selling the quilts without being caught. But here I go again, blaming them without any proof.

June 3

Garden goodies are on the menu—lettuce, baby carrots, radishes, spring onions, parsley, and sugar snap peas. Yum! We like the carrots and radishes on slices of buttered homemade bread. Yesterday I made four loaves of white bread, and it was cooling on the counter when there was a knock on the door. When I opened the door, the aroma of freshly baked bread must have wafted out, for the lady began to sniff and ooh and aahh over the wonderful smell (she had come to look at some hay we have for sale). She asked if she could buy some bread, and since it is best fresh anyway, I said she could. She followed me to the kitchen and selected two loaves. Next we'll have to start a bakery, too.

Jared had an unfortunate experience this afternoon on his pony cart. Kermit sent him to town on an errand, and when he was coming home, he saw the Bentley boys near Rocky Ridge. They came tearing through the woods on their four-wheeler and

came out on the road just behind him. Swerving out around Jared, the brothers began pelting him with eggs as fast as they could. Some of them missed, but enough hit the target that he was quite splattered with them.

Jared came home muttering dire and unreasonable threats, but after he was cleaned up and in a better frame of mind, he was able to listen to Kermit's advice. If only we could somehow turn those boys into friends instead of enemies.

Bethany was over tonight, and when she heard the story, she was properly disgusted. Her school is not out yet, and she said that Joey Bentley is still being mean to Elma, the plain girl who sits in front of him in class. The worst of it is, the teacher pretends not to see or know. Bethany said she thinks that Mrs. Helm is a friend of Mrs. Bentley. It doesn't sound good.

Tonight Kermit brought me a bouquet of wild roses from the fence row. He's always doing kind and thoughtful things for me. It reminds me of the verse that Sadie had written in the card she gave with our wedding gift, which I'll copy here:

May your wedded life be like the blooming roses
With a beauty given only from above,
Watered with the showers of the Saviour's blessing,
Growing in the sunshine of His gracious love.

June 5

Emily has been begging for a dress and apron just like mine, and since today was a rainy day I took the time to sit at the sewing machine and make her an outfit. She had a choice of plain green, brown, or lavender for the dress. She chose lavender and wanted the apron to match. That was okay. She again begged for an organdy *Kapp*, but I decided that just isn't necessary.

Emily's mom had given me permission to make an outfit for Emily, and she said she didn't care if Emily wears it while she is here. I thought that was real generous of her (I guess she knows we don't like short skirts or skimpy dresses). When the dress and apron were finished, Emily put them on and pranced around happily with Mini on her shoulder, and Mini looked about as pleased as Emily, with those dark little darting eyes gleaming merrily.

Ever since the Sunday evening I had popped a bowl of popcorn for a snack and Mini took to it like a raccoon does to a sweet corn patch, we like to keep some on hand. She simply dived into the bowl, scattering kernels everywhere—a wild orgy of delight for her. So when the rain was over and the sun came out, Emily, with her new outfit on, got a handful of buttered popcorn out of the canister we keep filled just for Mini and went out to show Kermit, Treva, and Jared, who were busy mulching the newly planted hybrid cantaloupe plants. Kermit told me later that Emily pirouetted and whirled around in front of them, happily showing off her new attire as though she was dressed like a queen. She is teaching Mini tricks—she holds up a kernel of corn and makes Mini sit up and beg with her front paws folded in front of her. It's so cute!

Tonight when Emily's mom came to pick her up, she still had her plain outfit on, and her mom ran out to the car for her camera. She took lots of pictures of Emily and Mini together, showing off the tricks she had learned, and said after the pictures were developed she would give us one, too. It will be a remembrance of Emily after we no longer have her here.

June 8

Love like pretty flowers
Needs to be given care;
Untended flowers wither
And seedlings will not bear.

I was reminded of this verse this morning when Emily came and wasn't her usual happy self. She moped around unhappily and was easily upset at the slightest little provocation. When Mini hid under the couch and refused to come out, Emily burst into tears and cried as if her heart would break. This is a common trick of the ferret's, and usually Emily likes to play hide and seek with her. So I knew that something more had to be bothering Emily—but what? I held and rocked her for awhile, and when she continued to sniffle, I asked her what was wrong.

She started to cry again and said brokenly, "My daddy moved out! I want my daddy to come back and live with us again. I don't want Mommy and Daddy to get a divorce."

Poor little girl. What could I say? Surely if such people realized the heartaches they create for their children, they would choose to forgive and to love unconditionally, and to have forbearance for each other's faults. All I could think to say was that maybe her daddy would come back soon. But the words had a hollow ring to them, for I could not reassure her that he would. I told her that I'm sure that both her mommy and her daddy still loved her and would take care of her, and how would she like for me and her to go for a ride on Jared's pony cart? Her tears were soon forgotten as she happily pulled Mini out from under the couch and begged to be allowed to take the ferret along. She was delighted when I said she could if she would hold on to her.

The Bentley boys were still in school, so we weren't worried about flying eggs. We drove up the trail into Rocky

Ridge, and Emily was happy and excited about the ride, apparently having forgotten her heartaches. The woods are beautiful and shady since the leaves are out on the trees, and the birds were singing with joyous abandon. I believe God made the birds with pretty songs to cheer people in this "sad world of sorrow and care," as the songwriter puts it.

We drove up to the Bryans' house, and though Bethany was at school, Mrs. Bryan welcomed us warmly into her house (ferret and all). She served us iced tea (the store-bought kind) and Twinkies. Emily played happily the rest of the day, and I'm so glad she was able to forget her heartache.

> ***Golden Gem for today**: Walk like Christ, and you shall always abide near Christ. The presence of Christ invites you to come and have unbroken fellowship with Him. To walk through all the circumstances and temptations of life is exactly like (Peter's) walking on the water—you have no solid ground under your feet, but you have the Word of God to rest on.*

June 9

This place has a lot of lovely flowers—first, the spring flowering bulbs, then there are buttercups, wild roses, meadowsweets, and forget-me-nots, all in their own time. And then the annuals I planted—petunias, sweet allysiums, marigolds, firebranch, snapdragons, begonias, and impatiens. Kermit knows I love flowers and often brings in a bouquet or, rather, just a sprig or two.

But we've already found out that it's not all roses, for oftentimes life is filled with cares perplexing, with storm clouds as well as sunshine. I quake to think of the mistake I nearly made this afternoon. A very dear and sweet silver-haired lady was here (Mom Mullet had sent her, since I had her quilts over here), hoping to be able to select a quilt that suited her as a gift for her daughter-in-law. She chose a Broken Star quilt, all in shades of blue, and seemed very happy with it. She paid with three $100 bills plus a twenty-dollar bill to cover the tax. I had to go to the kitchen to get two dollars change, and when she asked to use the bathroom, I told her to follow me.

I laid the $320 on the kitchen table and went to the desk for the two dollars change. While I had my back turned, she stood beside the table admiring the grain on the old knotty pine cabinet in the corner. After I had given the woman her change, I showed her where the bathroom is, then went to put my money away.

I gasped when I saw there were only two $100 bills left there, besides the twenty-dollar bill. What had become of the other $100 bill? There on the table was the lady's pocketbook. Could she possibly have taken it?

Without stopping to think what I was doing, I opened her purse. Oh, no! There, on top of everything else, lay the $100 bill. Would it be all right to take it and say nothing about it? For a moment I wavered, struggling with indecision. She must have taken it, I reasoned, for what else could have happened to it? Was she a wolf in sheep's clothing, a sneaky thief? Slowly I closed her purse again, for something told me that no way would it be right for me to steal her $100, even though she might have stolen from me.

When the lady came back into the kitchen, the first thing she said was, "What's that lying under the table? It looks like money."

And it was—the missing $100 bill! A feeling of hot shame washed over me for what I had nearly done. What would that dear lady have thought had she later found her $100 missing out of her purse? I wouldn't even have known her name to contact her about it later. I blush to think about it. *Ya well*, that's one thing I won't tell Kermit, and I learned a lesson from it. All's well that ends well.

June 13

Jared and Treva made a scarecrow for the garden yesterday to keep the pesky sparrows and blackbirds away. Snickers thought it was a stranger, so he barked and barked at it most of the afternoon. Emily tried to tell him it was only a scarecrow, but, of course, it did no good. Finally, we penned him up in the carriage shed so we would have some peace and quiet.

Sometime last night (I was only half awake) I thought I heard Snickers barking again, dimly aware that he must have

somehow gotten out and was again barking at Mr. Scarecrow. I drifted off again, only to be awakened for real by Snickers' urgent barking, joined by Rindy.

Muttering dire threats, Kermit jumped out of bed, got dressed, and went out to check. I went to the window, thinking it might help if I would tell Snickers and Rindy to be quiet. By the light of the moon I saw the outline of the barn, chicken house, and carriage shed. Down in the meadow was a pool of moonlight, and in looking closer, I thought I saw a person moving around.

I strained my eyes, trying to see if it was just a cow or stray dog. The cloud parted a bit, and yes, it was a person crouched low and sneaking! He straightened up then, and began to run, headed in the direction of Rocky Ridge. I watched until he disappeared into the darkness and shadows of the trees in the meadow. The dogs were still barking, then I saw an orange glow behind the barn, and a flickering light reflected against the chicken house. Fire!

I dressed faster than I ever had before and woke Jared and Treva, who were up in a jiffy and not far behind me in running outside. Behind the barn, Kermit was scooping water out of the horse's water trough as fast as he could, trying to douse the flames that were creeping up the side of the "peepie house" (where baby chicks had been kept years ago), as we call the little shed behind the barn. He had the spigot open to refill the trough and we quickly formed a bucket brigade. Jared wanted to call the fire department, but Kermit thought we could handle it ourselves. And, thankfully, we did.

Snickers' barking had saved the barn, chicken house, and carriage shed as well, for they are close to each other. Kermit remarked that whoever had left Snickers out of his pen is a real hero. No one claimed to have done it, and upon checking, we discovered the door to the carriage house was still locked. There was an open window, though, five feet about ground, which Snickers must have jumped out. He is a real hero!

We were unable to sleep much the rest of the night after all that excitement. I waited until Treva and Jared were back in bed to tell Kermit about the shadowy figure I saw running toward Rocky Ridge. We decided it must have been one of the Bentleys. There was no evidence of arson in the peepie house, but it might have burned away. I hope we'll be able to get to the bottom of it and, if it was the Bentley boys again, unveil the cause and root of their hostility.

June 14

Kermit and Chuck are real cowboys these days, herding the Herefords into new grazing areas, roping and branding the calves, and sorting the older ones. At night they come in bone tired and covered with dust. It's dangerous, too, for the range bulls aren't to be trusted. Silver is a trained cattle horse, and so is Chuck's stallion, Ayers. Both are experts at dodging charging cattle, but still, I'll be very thankful when it's over.

Kermit's mom and Stephanie stopped in this afternoon, and both of them were quite friendly. Stephanie is really very nice now that I'm getting to know her. It sure is an answer to prayer. They both admired the inspirational calendar I made and thought it was a lovely gift. Stephanie is interested in learning to quilt. She started going to quilting classes in Little Falls, so she wanted to see all the new quilts that Mom Mullet had sent over. It was a happy afternoon and we parted as friends. It's such a good feeling even though we are not of the same faith.

June 15

From my kitchen window I saw Kermit riding Silver down over the knob, going after a group of stray cattle. I'm not sure how it happened, but the next time I looked, Kermit was on the ground and an angry-looking range bull was towering over him, snorting through his nostrils and pawing the dirt and bellowing his rage. He tossed Kermit up into the air a couple of times before Kermit was able to roll into the center of a scrub thicket. I ran outside screaming for Chuck.

In a short time Chuck was racing to the scene in his Jeep, going to Kermit's rescue. All the while the angry bull was attacking the thicket, trying to get at Kermit while he crouched there. The bull's horns kept tangling in the vines and thorns, and I think that's what saved Kermit.

With the Jeep, Chuck managed to lure the bull away, and then he sped back to rescue Kermit. In a few minutes they were safely on the other side of the fence, with the gate barred. Chuck helped Kermit into the house where he spent the rest of the day on the sofa. He says he is all right, except it feels like there are a few ribs either cracked or broken. We hardly spoke a word to each other all afternoon, we were that shaken.

By evening we were ready to talk, and Kermit said he's been doing some deep thinking. The preacher at the last service spoke of being lukewarm. He quoted Scripture, "Because thou art neither hot nor cold, I will spew thee out of my mouth." Kermit said he thinks he's been a lukewarm Christian—not all that sincere, and when that big brute had him at his mercy, Kermit knew that he didn't want to continue like that.

I confessed my own spiritual laxness, too, and together we pledged our whole hearts to the Lord. There is so much to learn of the Christian life, and so many real life lessons to learn. We are not promised even one more day, and if we live our lives in self-seeking and sin, someday it will be too late.

Part Three

Summertime at Tall Cedars

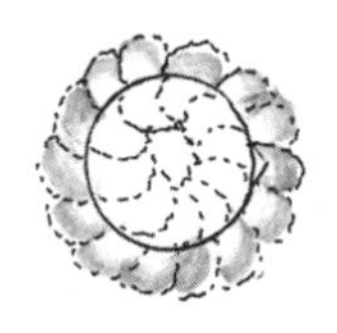

June 25 (Sunday)

This evening it was rather nice to be alone for a change with no *maud* and *gnecht* here. Emily had taken Mini the ferret along home for the weekend, for her mother has gotten used to him. We attended church services this morning and were at Rachel and Ben's for a visit before we came home. I wonder why Rachel's dreams are coming true and mine are not. I know Kermit would make such a good daddy. But we know God knows best; we don't want to fret about it. Tonight we sat on the porch reminiscing, and even planning for the future.

The rose bush that Kermit gave me for my birthday still has a single blooming rose on it, and it is just perfect. If only it could last! But then it wouldn't be real.

Later we went for a walk in the meadow and saw a mother duck with ten cute, downy ducklings following her, swimming along the reeds near the bank. We walked farther than we ever had before and discovered an old waterwheel which stands dilapidated and unused; it makes a nice old-fashioned picture. A muskrat has his home nearby, and a long-legged heron landed on the opposite bank. All was serene and peaceful, but it wasn't hard to imagine the old waterwheel in working condition, with the water turning the paddles, creaking continually.

A pair of screech owls hooted from a tree in the woods. We sat on a fallen log until we could glimpse the new moon, just a sliver of silver visible through the pines and cedars. The fragrance of the wild roses on the opposite bank was sweet, and the sleepy murmurings of the birds as they settled for the night gave the evening an air of peacefulness and tranquility.

It will be hard to leave this place for we're getting attached to it, and our memories are good ones, but we know we can't stay. Some day we'll look back with nostalgia and longing to our

days on our "honeymoon" homestead. I think I'll have time to copy a verse yet before Kermit comes in from the barn.

> **Golden Gem for today:** *Faith is that meekness of soul which waits in stillness to hear, to understand, to accept what God says, to receive, to retain, to possess what God gives. By faith we allow God to become our very life. And, because holiness is God's highest glory and blessing, it is especially in the life of holiness that we need to live by faith alone.*

June 26

Emily's cherished little pet, Mini the ferret, became sick today. She wouldn't eat but just curled up in her little nest-lined box behind the wood stove and refused to come out to play, in spite of Emily's pleading. She was very listless, and Emily was so distraught tonight when her dad came to pick her up that he promised to take Mini to the vet for him to try and make her well. Oh, dear, I wonder who's going to pay for that. But we can't let her suffer without doing something for her.

We are having very warm weather so I didn't make much for supper. Kermit drove into town for a sack of crushed ice and I made custard for strawberry ice cream. Kermit cranked the ice cream freezer. Bossy the cow gives plenty of cream, so it wasn't exactly the non-fat kind. Ben and Rachel came over and we all sat on the porch eating delicious and refreshing strawberry ice cream along with the Auntie Anne's soft pretzels Rachel had brought along.

Art and Delphine drove in, too, just in time to share the treat, and stayed until bedtime. They hit if off well and everyone was visiting together and having a good time, just like old friends. *Make new friends but keep the old. The one is silver and the other is gold.*

Ben and Rachel were ready to leave and had just untied the green-broke colt they were driving and climbed on the buggy when Snickers bounded over to them, scaring the horse. He reared up on his hind legs and stood poised for a moment while we held our breaths, afraid that he would fall over. But then, in a moment he was on all fours again and heading out the lane in a flurry of gravel. Whew! I'm glad our Patsy is better behaved than that. With all the traffic on the road these days, it is dangerous enough even when our horse is reliable.

July 20

My big batch of sweet corn was ready today, and I felt fortunate to have such good help—Treva and Jared. Kermit and Jared brought in a spring wagon load of it, and we all sat under the big pine tree in the back yard husking it, then brushing off the silk and cutting the kernels into dishpans. Emily likes to eat raw corn right off the cob, and Snickers would too if we let him. While we worked, we visited and told stories, so it wasn't nearly as tiresome as tackling the job alone would have been. Many hands make light work.

Kermit told a few stories, things that had happened in his childhood years, and even a few I'd never heard before. Kermit must not always have been as good as he is now, for I learned that in second grade he had once played hookey and gone fishing instead of going to school as he was supposed to. Another time when he was supposed to cut up a bushel of potatoes, he had gotten the brilliant idea of planting the potatoes whole instead of cutting them in pieces, so it would go faster.

I tattled on myself, too, and told about the time (when I was nine years old) I swept the dust and dirt under the *Sitzschtubb* rug for a whole month instead of sweeping it up. Then when we had a roomful of company, Mom had lifted the rug to show one of the aunts how it was made—be sure your sins will find you out! Treva really laughed about that and agreed that at age nine I was old enough to know better.

The kitchen was too warm and steamy from canning, so when the last jar was lifted out of the canner, we headed for the creek to cool off and to eat our picnic supper. It was blessedly cooler there, so peaceful and refreshing. I had made a deep-dish pizza and Treva made a scrumptious salad. We had a blueberry pie and, of course, plenty of frosty, cold meadow tea. We'll be glad when the watermelons are ready. Chuck joined our party, too. Treva and Jared helped to carry the food and blankets to sit on. Everyone agreed that it was too warm to start a bonfire for roasting marshmallows. We all had a very lovely evening.

Heat lightning flickered far above the mountains and we heard a few low rumblings of thunder every now and then, but nothing came of it. Kermit, Jared, and Treva went wading in the river and I sat on the bank, dangling my feet in the water and talking to Chuck and Rindy. Snickers sniffed out bunny trails and tried to dig a groundhog out of his den, but finally gave up and joined the ones in the creek, enjoying the splashing and playing. Birds twittered sleepily from the treetops, a few squawking night herons flew overhead, and frogs croaked from the shallows. It was an evening to store in our treasure chest of precious memories. I think I'll copy a verse from the "Love at Home" song:

> *Kindly Heaven smiles above, When there's love at home.*
> *All the earth is filled with love, When there's love at home.*
> *Sweeter sings the brooklet by, Brighter beams the azure sky.*
> *Oh, there's one who smiles on high, When there's love at home.*

July 21

A heavy thunderstorm and two inches of rain last night finally dispersed the heat wave, and, oh, what a difference it makes! It's twenty degrees cooler and the humidity evaporated, giving one a feeling of boundless energy and goodwill. I'm glad to get a taste of this kind of weather, because that heat wave made me listless.

Emily had to shed a few tears when I told her that Mini wasn't feeling the best again, so the ferret will get more attention and will probably be taken to the vet. Mrs. Bryan and Bethany came down tonight and cheered us up by their friendliness. We played a game of croquet out on the front lawn—something that just wouldn't have been enjoyable at all during our heat wave.

Later, sitting on the porch rockers, swing, and glider, it was actually chilly, and so nice. I guess it's good we don't always have pleasant weather, so we don't take it for granted when we do have it. We sat and visited until late, feeling thankful for the lovely weather we had and all the memories.

> ***Thought for today:*** *Friendship is a joy to be shared and cherished. Someday there will be no more farewells, in the sweet by and by.*

August 3

Treva and Jared help Chuck out in the fields a lot of the time, doing whatever is necessary each day. I am usually in the kitchen, busy canning whatever is ripe, or working in the garden or yard. This afternoon I mixed an angel food cake and had just popped it into the oven when Kermit came in and asked if I could help him in the shop for a few minutes, handing him tools while he crawled underneath the feed mixer, making repairs.

Yes, of course I would, and when that was finished, I stayed to chat while he worked at blacking Patsy's harness. On the way to the house, I noticed that the petunias I'd planted around the big stump beside the cattle pen needed weeding, so I did that.

Back at the kitchen, I was greeted at the door with the aroma of something burning. Oh, dear! My beautiful angel food cake was burned black! And Kermit came in for a drink just then and had to see it all. What a poor housekeeper he must have thought me! But he kindly took the blame upon himself for having asked me to help him. I had to think of the following verse in my poem book:

Love is not blind—
It sees more, not less,
But because it sees more
It is willing to see less.

Less of the other's faults and mistakes, I suppose it means, or rather, to overlook them and to forgive. Also, to—

Tend love with understanding
Feed it with tenderness
Sincerity, and sacrifice.
Give love a thousand tender smiles.

August 8

My journal writing ambition is waning lately, mostly because there are so many other things to be done. It is hard to believe that autumn is fast approaching, and that it's soon time for school to start again. Both Treva's and Jared's parents have given their permission for us to keep our *Maad* and *Gnecht* over the coming school term. All this came about because Bethany Bryan doesn't want to travel to her school on the school bus anymore because of a fallout she had with Joey Bentley. So Mrs. Bryan will be driving Bethany to school every morning and picking her up in the evening. She goes right by Treva and Jared's parochial school and is willing to take them along and drop them off there. We are all very happy about this arrangement, and it's good to know that Treva and Jared like working for us and want to stay.

When the busy fall season with its harvesting and canning is over, I plan to piece quilts for Mom Mullet to sell (to quilt them, too). Treva can quilt very nicely and it will keep us busy over the winter months when the snow flies. Kermit plans to put together cedar chests from kits for a local craftsman, and Jared will help in the evening after the chores are done.

This afternoon Emily and I went for elderberries from the bushes growing along the creek banks. Snickers bounded along, too, scaring the bunnies out of the thickets and the fat old woodchuck that has its den under a rock pile. Emily waded into the water in the shallow part of the creek, tossing pebbles at the darting minnows, watching the ripples form and disappear, while I filled my baskets. We're having warm weather again, but it was pleasantly cool there compared to anywhere else.

I made five elderberry pies and as usual, they cooked out a bit and I had to scrub the oven, but they were good and worth all the trouble. Our homemade strawberry ice cream had made us hungry for more, and Kermit brought another bag of crushed ice and rock salt along from town. After I'd gotten the ingredients ready, he cranked the two-quart freezer while the elderberry pies cooled. We made vanilla this time, and it sure "goes good" with *hollerbiere* (elderberry) pie, especially in this kind of weather.

We ate out in the back yard under the trees since the kitchen was warm from baking pies. I noticed that the weeds are taking over in the garden. With the bounteous rains we've been having, the weeds just run wild.

Jared hitched his pony to his cart and drove over to his cousin's pond to go swimming. I almost wished I was a carefree girl myself and could go for a swim, too. But there were a lot of elderberries waiting to be canned in the steamy kitchen. I'm not complaining—just explaining.

August 30

Our hearts ache so for Rachel and Ben tonight. Today we attended graveside services for their stillborn twin sons. There were complications that I don't understand which took the lives of the healthy-looking, full term (but tiny) babies. They looked so sweet and peaceful, side by side in the little coffin, almost as if they were only sleeping and that if someone would just pick them up and hold them, they would awaken and smile sweet angelic smiles and their little dimpled hands would come to life, to be kissed and cuddled.

I think it was almost merciful that Rachel couldn't be there to see her darlings being lowered into the tiny grave. But then, Ben had to face it alone, without his helpmeet at his side. I feel very guilty now about the pangs of envy I had felt at times, for I think it would have been worse to have been harboring dreams and anticipation all these months and then have them dashed to the ground.

But it's good to remember that the babies are "safe in the arms of Jesus," never to know any sin and strife. By and by the heartache will lessen and fade, for most likely other little ones will come to grace their home and cheer their hearts.

The Mullets stopped in tonight on their way home from visiting shut-ins and stayed for supper. We talked about Aunt Miriam and Uncle Nate's Amanda, who died when she was just four. Mom said she thinks that the longer one is allowed to have a child, the harder it is to give him up. That's not so hard to understand, although Rachel might not find it so easy to believe just now. We must remember to pray for her.

> ***Golden Gem for today:*** *Faith accepts the promise in its divine reality. Hope goes forward to examine and rejoice in the treasures which faith has accepted. Faith will perhaps be most tried when God wants most to bless. Hope is the daughter of faith, the messenger it sends out to see what is to come. It is hope that becomes the strength and support of faith.*

September 9

Clear, crisp autumn-like days are here, and the grapes are hanging purple on the vine. Silo filling will soon begin, along with wild geese flying south, apple picking and cider making, housecleaning, long with the wedding season.

We had visitors tonight. Jill and Wynn, the newlywed couple, came and ordered another wall hanging for their new home. They talked about their honeymoon trip and what fun they had swimming in the ocean, surfboarding, exploring the beach, and sailing. It made us almost feel as though we had missed something grand. But I guess there's a reason that pleasure trips are disapproved of among our people, for they are of no benefit to the soul.

September 10 (Sunday)

Some of the leaves on the trees are starting to change color already; soon there will be some lovely scenery over in Rocky Ridge. Kermit and I walked out to it this evening, and on up to Lookout Point. We were the only ones there, so the peace and beauty of our surroundings were undisturbed.

On the way back we stopped at the abandoned house and decided to climb the ladder to the second floor where the stolen quilts had been hidden. There was nothing amiss up there and we found no stolen loot.

Just as we were walking back to the trail, we heard that dreaded sound—the roar of the four-wheeler coming down the trail. We quickly ran back into the old house and pulled the door shut. But as the vehicle came closer, it began to slow down and swerved up the path to the old house. Two boys walked up to the old house and yanked open the door. Seeing us inside, they began to yell angrily and wave their fists.

We escaped through the sagging back door. We had to cross the boggy old spring, and my foot slipped off a rock and I stepped into the water. It appeared to be shallow, but there was some thick mud underneath.

Kermit was saying, "Hurry, Joy," but my foot was stuck and I could not budge it. He tried to pull me out by the arm; finally, my shoe came off and I was free. We crept through the woods until we found a trail that led homeward. When we were out on the road, a carriage passed us and I'm sure they wondered why I had on only one shoe.

Our walk was spoiled, but I'm sure leaving was the best thing to do, even though it may have appeared cowardly. If the boys would have resorted to rock throwing, they would have gotten the best of us anyway. It was better to avoid a scene.

Bible verse for today: *"But I say unto you, Love your enemies, bless them that curse you, do good to them that hate you, and pray for them which despitefully use you and persecute you; that ye may be the children of your father which is in Heaven: for He maketh his sun to rise on the evil and on the good, and sendeth rain on the just and on the unjust." (Matthew 5:44-45)*

September 11

Treva and Jared have a lot of interesting school stories to talk about in the evenings, and it sure brings back memories of my school days. In the morning they pack their lunches—usually sandwiches, an apple, bunches of grapes, pretzels, jars of chocolate milk, and sometimes Thermos bottles of soup. They hop on their scooters and go a mile down the road to the end of the Bryans' lane, which is near the far end of Rocky Ridge. This saves Mrs. Bryan four miles of driving in a day, two in the morning and two in the evening.

But they've run into a bit of a problem, for the Bentley boys are usually out at the end of their lane, waiting for the bus that takes them to their high school. It seems they'll do whatever they can to create a hardship for Treva and Jared, be it hollering taunts and threats, or tossing stones, etc. Kermit told them they ought to think of some way to heap "coals of fire" upon their heads, returning kindness for contempt, but they haven't been able to think of anything yet.

Bethany has stories to tell about her school, too, whenever she comes over. She says that Joey Bently is again harassing Elma this year, too. She's usually very indignant about how her teacher, Mrs. Helm, conveniently doesn't see or notice when Joey harasses Elma. She said she would just love to give Joey what is due him, if the teacher doesn't. I try to remind them (although it's hard for me to grasp this truth, too) that revenge never pays; it hurts the one who indulges in it more than the victim. I also tell them that backbiting is unchristian. I guess sometimes we all long to put the "an eye for an eye, and a tooth for a tooth" philosophy into use, although it's better to "pray for them which despitefully use you," as the Bible says.

Part Four

Autumntime at Tall Cedars

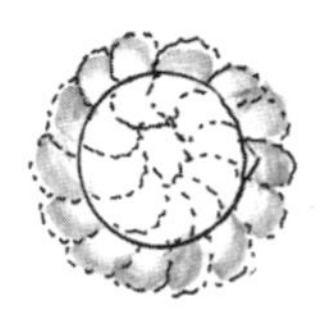

October 4

Emily was all smiles when her mother brought her this morning. She said, “My daddy came back to live with us again.” Her eyes shone with happiness, and I was so glad for her. She seems almost like one of the family now—I just wish she **would** belong to us. She’s using more and more Dutch words. It won’t be long until she can speak it fluently. With her dress and apron just like mine, she looks like a plain girl.

I spent most of the day raking leaves under the big maple trees and some under the oak and beech trees, too. Emily loved to gleefully jump into the piles of leaves, followed by Mini, the little ferret. Snickers was too rambunctious, scattering leaves everywhere, so I penned her in the carriage shed.

Just before supper we had a rather unusual visitor (Treva and Bethany were out in the field with Kermit and Jared, picking broccoli heads for market). The lady wanted to order a Country Bride appliqued quilt; luckily, I had one already made (by Mom) that suited her. When she was ready to pay, I told her the total with the tax included.

At the mention of the word “tax,” the woman drew herself up haughtily and snapped, “How can you ask me to pay tax? You people don’t pay your taxes.” She flung the money down on the counter, turned on her heel, and stormed out the door. Too stunned to make a reply, I just stood there in astonishment for awhile.

A short time later the door opened and Bethany came in with an armload of broccoli heads. “What did Mrs. Helm want here?” she asked. “She didn’t look like she was in a very good mood when I passed her.”

Ahhh . . . so that was Bethany’s teacher, the one who took Joey Bentley’s side at school! Slowly I began to put two and two together, for I had gotten an inkling of the cause of her and the Bentleys’ hostility. Hadn’t Treva said that Mrs. Helm was a friend to Mrs. Bentley? Maybe it’s time to have a talk with them both to clear up some misconceptions.

A plan began to form in my mind, but I didn't know whether or not it would do any good. This evening after the others were in bed, I told the entire story to Kermit and sounded out my ideas to him. If Mrs. Helm and the Bentleys were mad at us because they had the mistaken idea that we didn't pay taxes, wasn't it time to do something about it? We talked until late, then decided that the best thing to do would be to talk to someone older and wiser about it first. We went to bed then, but sleep was slow in coming, for it wasn't a very good feeling to think about: a lot of people might be angry and resentful, blaming us for not paying taxes. Ach, my, no wonder the Bentley boys had been trying their best to make life difficult for us.

November 1

Snow flurries this morning heralded the coming of winter, and also the wedding season. I attended an all-day quilting today at Rachel and Ben's house and got caught up on all the community news. Rachel had two quilts in frames and both quilts were filled, so there was good attendance.

We had a carry-in covered dish dinner, a scrumptious spread of good variety. Why does other people's cooking taste so much better than my own? There was a big casserole of "chicken in a crumb basket," a kettle full of chicken pot pie, a pizza casserole, a roast pan full of scalloped corn, and several salads. For dessert there was cherry cream cheese delight, blueberry pies, graham cracker vanilla fluff, pumpkin whoopie pies, and fruit salad.

Rachel seems to be back to her usual cheerful self, although I know there must be an ache in her heart that will never leave. Especially when other mothers come with their darling little bundles, or when the mothers' conversations are mostly about their babies and the joys and cares of motherhood. I feel left out, too, but I keep reminding myself that it's only temporary, or at least I hope so.

Mom was there, too, and I was able to have a talk with her alone. I told her all about what Mrs. Helm said to us and about the Bentleys' hostility. Kermit talked to his accountant last week and he's working in our favor to help clear up misunderstandings and false rumors. We're just waiting now to see what happens.

November 12 (Sunday)

No church today, and with the warm, balmy weather and some golden leaves still floating peacefully down from the trees, we couldn't resist going for a walk in Rocky Ridge this afternoon, hoping we wouldn't meet up with any of the Bentley crew.

Blue jays were calling from the treetops and a noisy flock of crows serenaded us. The forest floor under the trees was scattered with acorns, shellbarks, and hazelnuts. The squirrels were busy, chattering noisily while scampering here and there, gathering nuts for their winter storehouses. The autumn smell of wood smoke was in the air.

We went for a drive this afternoon, and at several places we could see people taking advantage of the lovely day, working in the yards raking leaves. Someone was burning leaves in a field. It's a bit hard to get used to, seeing people working on a Sunday.

Everything seemed so calm and peaceful there in the woods and we were fast beginning to think that the Bentleys must all be away. It was with a feeling of dismay that we heard the engine of a four-wheeler revving up, and a few minutes later it came around a curve in the path. But, lo and behold, when the boy driving it saw us, he slowed down and passed us quite respectfully (we had stepped aside out of the path). He passed with a smile and a wave of his hand. It was none other than Joey Bentley!

It was quite a surprise to us that he had tried to be friendly—a pleasant surprise! We had another surprise coming, for a lady came hiking down the trail then and stopped for a friendly chat. She introduced herself as Mrs. Bentley and seemed to be a very decent and amiable woman. She asked if it was true that her boys had thrown rocks at us once, and when we answered in the affirmative, she apologized profusely and assured us she would see to it that it wouldn't happen again; we would be treated with respect after this. We parted as friends, thankful that our prayers had been answered.

Next, Bethany Bryan came riding down the trail on her painted pony; when we told her the good news, she rejoiced with us. She said that Joey Bentley has changed at school, too, and is treating Elma with new respect. We can't help but wonder what brought about the change in their attitude and whether Mrs. Helm had something to do with it. If so, what made her change her mind? I hope we'll find out soon.

November 15

Today is our first anniversary, although the weather is a bit nicer today than it was a year ago. It brought back a lot of memories!

Tonight Kermit made supper all by himself for a change. He told me to sit on the rocker while he did all the work! He made potato soup, hot dogs, egg salad, and set out grape jam and chocolate whoopie pies for dessert. He whipped some cream for a topping for the jam, too. He even washed all the dishes by himself, not even allowing me to as much as dry them. How sweet and thoughtful of him!

November 24 (Thanksgiving Day)

We had our "family" get-together at the Mullets and it was a very enjoyable day. Mom had roasted a big turkey to a golden brown perfection; stuffed with filling and giblets, it was the best I had ever tasted. Ben and Rachel were there, too, and she brought delicious gourmet potatoes, a first for us, and the vegetables and salad. Mom also had made the desserts, except for the pecan and pumpkin pies, which I had made.

In the afternoon we were treated to "Buck Eyes" (kiddie food). I guess I shouldn't have said it that way, because the adults liked them, too. Recipe follows.

Buck Eyes

2 cups Rice Krispies
1 cup crunchy peanut butter
1 cup 10x sugar
1/4 cup melted butter
dipping chocolate

Add dipping chocolate to ingredients. Mix everything together. Press and roll into balls, and dip in melted chocolate. Delicious!

We had a good time visiting this afternoon, and with Grandpa Mullet in a story-telling mood, the day passed quickly. He told about the time when he and his two brothers were still preschoolers, and his mother had to spend several weeks in bed. A young *Maad* came to do the work and care for the children. The three little boys were a handful, and the girl was young and inexperienced. He didn't remember what mischief they had gotten into, but after awhile her patience was tried to the limit. She tied the three little boys to a tree, then went to work in the garden, thinking the boys were safely out of mischief.

The boys grew tired of sitting there, and on seeing that the *Maad* had tied them only by their pants, they quickly slipped out of their pants and were free. They ran down to the brook in the meadow where their dad found them, happily splashing and playing in the water. From then on, he made it a point to take the boys with him until their mother was up and around again.

This also reminded Grandpa of the winter he was in first grade and had trouble with walking in his sleep. One evening he got the notion to tie his foot to the bedpost. But the next morning when he woke up, he found himself lying out in the yard beside the gatepost with his foot tied to it. He must have untied and retied it in his sleep. After that his mother kept the outside doors locked, and Grandpa soon got over his sleepwalking.

We stayed at the Mullets for a supper of leftovers, then played Pictionary with the youngsters. Ben and Rachel had stayed, too. We'll have to remember to cherish (and not take for granted) these times of togetherness, because someday we might move away and then we'll have nothing but the memories (and letters, of course).

> ***Golden Gem for today (Thanksgiving Day):***
> *To be thankful for what we've received and for what our Lord has prepared is the surest way to receive more. A joyful, thankful Christian shows that God can make those who serve Him truly happy. He stirs up others to praise God along with him.*

November 29

November has been a beautiful month this year, with lots of Indian summer weather. Harvest time is over, with the barn, corn crib, and granary well filled now. The cellar shelves are well stocked, the jars filled with summer and fall fruits and vegetables, all ready for the wintry snowstorms. Peace and plenty, home and hearth.

Wedding season is at its end, too—we attended four here in this district. It doesn't seem like a whole year since our big day! Our anniversary gifts to each other were a bit late because we were so busy earlier. Kermit presented me with a lovely miniature cedar chest he had made. Inside was a note that said:

Help our love for each other
To continue to bloom
As the day we became
A new bride and groom.

I had made a new shirt as a gift for him, so I quickly copied a verse for him and put it into the shirt pocket before I gave it:

What matters where our path will lead
How great the task, how much the need.
We trust in Jesus, strong and true,
And He will always see us through.

I suppose it may sound a bit sentimental to still be exchanging notes and gifts, but in seeing others' marriages, I see that there is a tendency to take each other for granted after awhile. Sometimes it's not until one partner is taken away, claimed by death, that the realization comes of how they were cherished. Sometimes people don't realize a blessing until it is gone.

December 1

We had a much appreciated visit last night from two fine ladies: Mrs. Helm and Mrs. Bentley. They had a bit of explaining to do, and they apologized for how they had misjudged us. Kermit's accountant had called Mrs. Helm and set her straight. In this day and age it wouldn't be easy for anyone to get out of filing tax, even if they had intentions of being dishonest, and even if they would have no income. There might have been a few who didn't start filing right away after it became law and mandatory, but that was soon done away with.

Both of the ladies were very much interested in the quilt I have in the frame, a queen-sized, appliquéd Country Love quilt in shades of rose and green. Mrs. Bentley said that if I have it finished by Christmas, she would like to buy it to give it to her sister. So that's a goal to work for, and with Treva's help I should be able to make it.

We had our first real snow last night, which makes it all the cozier to sit and work at the quilt. Our Tall Cedars Homestead is now covered with a blanket of beautiful, white and drifted snow; the spruce trees are a thing of loveliness, laden with mounds and swirls of it, and the fence posts have white caps. Emily spent a lot of time outdoors today and I must admit, I spent a good bit of time with her, helping her to make a big snowman, and also making a slick slide down the barn hill (by tramping down the snow and pouring water on it) for her to slide down on her sled. Treva and Jared took a few rides on it, too, when they came home from school. Tonight after the children were in their beds, Kermit and I went sledding, too. The moonlight glittered on the gleaming snow, making it sparkle and seem almost light as day. We wished we would have a horse-drawn sleigh here, but since we don't, we'll have to use the bobsled.

Jingle bells, jingle bells,
Jingle all the way.
Oh, what fun it would be to ride
In a one-horse open sleigh.

December 15

Today we started making Christmas goodies, much to Emily's delight. She mixed the buck-eye centers and helped roll them into balls, while I dipped them in the melted chocolate. From now until Christmas Day our house will probably be filled with the delightful smells of things cooking and baking. I'd like to have the Christmas family gathering here, because we might be moving later.

This afternoon before it was time to start supper and the chores, Emily and I went for a walk in the meadow. We had had a fresh dusting of snow again and wanted to take in all that pristine loveliness. Following the creek, we saw the dainty paw prints of little

woodland folks such as rabbits, mice, and birds. I taught Emily how to make an angel imprint by lying on her back in the soft snow and sweeping her arms wide, in a semi-circle. She's like a real snow hare, diving into drifts, and turning somersaults over them. But she stays snug and cozy—she has a coverall snowsuit with a furry collar and hood and only her nose and eyes are exposed.

We visited the barn, too, where it's always warm and cozy. Bossy the cow lowed gently, then contentedly went on chewing her cud. The horses nickered questioningly, probably wondering why we were there when it wasn't feeding time. Mitsy, the cat Emily claims for her special pet, came purring around our legs and meowing inquiringly. Emily loves it in the barn, but she always misses chore time because she is not here early enough and doesn't stay that late.

Outside the barn a row of icicles made a pretty fringe along the roof. Snickers came bounding out of his doghouse, wagging his tail and wiggling all over with delight. I think we can say he is our dog now, for in spite of our advertising in the lost and found column, no one ever came to claim him. We made another snowman in the front yard, then headed back for the cheery warmth of the kitchen, I to sit at my quilt and stitch away, and Emily to play with Mini the ferret. Tonight we want to begin wrapping Christmas presents.

> ***Golden Gem for today:*** *We should learn to say, "The less I can spend on myself and the more on the Lord, the richer I am." Day by day, give, as God blesses and as He asks. It will help to bring Heaven nearer to you and you nearer to Heaven.*

December 19

Brrr! What a cold winter twilight this is! The snow has blown into shallow drifts and sleet is rattling against the window panes. At least it's snug and warm here in the kitchen, with the inviting smell of freshly-made doughnuts still lingering. There's beef roasting in the Gem-Pak and as soon as I open the door its delicious aroma fills the kitchen as well.

Rachel spent the day here, and what an enjoyable day it was! She is always an inspiration to me, with her cheerful acceptance of whatever betides, and her generous, unselfish personality. We made divinity fudge, besides the doughnuts, and cracked hickory nuts for the cake I plan to bake tomorrow. She made the gingerbread for her candy-covered and frosted gingerbread house. She said she makes it every year, then takes it along to the Christmas Day gathering for the youngsters to admire and enjoy. We're going to have Emily with us on Christmas Day—in fact, from Christmas until New Year, because her mother is taking a trip to Hawaii (by jet) over that time and leaving Emily here.

We got a Christmas card from Jill and Wynn, so they haven't forgotten us yet. I think I'll write a long letter to them tonight.

This evening Kermit and I read the Christmas story and were reminded of the real meaning of Christmas—celebrating Christ's birth. Without His sacrifice, life would be a cheerless and meaningless existence.

> ***Verse for today:*** *"And the angel said unto them, Fear not: for, behold, I bring you good tidings of great joy, which shall be to all people. For unto you is born this day in the city of David a Saviour, which is Christ the Lord." (Luke 2:10, 11)*

December 25

Christmas Day, and we had our family gathering here in spite of a gently falling snow that lasted most of the day. Things didn't go so well for me in preparing the meal. The turkey wasn't quite as tender as it should have been and the filling wasn't as tasty as Mom's was on Thanksgiving Day. One of the Mullet children spilled a pitcher of water all over the table, soaking a plate of sliced homemade bread, but at least we had plenty more. The gravy had a few lumps, which probably no one but me noticed, and the hickory nut cake sagged a bit on one side. But Kermit said tonight that the meal was real scrumptious and he thought I was the best cook in three counties, so I felt a lot better.

Emily was here, too, and she had the time of her life playing in the snow with the others, making a snow fort and sliding on the barn hill. Treva and Jared spent the day at their own homes, taking in their family gatherings.

Mom Mullet's gingerbread house was a big hit. The children were allowed to pick off candy canes and gumdrops. I think I can say that everyone had an enjoyable day, although Emily wondered why we didn't have a Christmas tree. I told her that we have our Christmas trees outside, decorated with snow.

Oh, yes, I forgot to write about the cookie exchange we had last Thursday. A group of ten (friends and relatives) got together at Rachel's house, each with ten dozen cookies of one kind, then we exchanged and traded until each had ten different kinds. There were walnut kisses, cherry macaroons, snowman hats, chocolate chip cookies, peanut butter cups, raisin-filled, sand tarts, chocolate marshmallow and frosted sugar cookies, and date rolls. It was quite a variety, and all were delicious. That should keep Kermit happy for awhile since he likes cookies with his morning cup of coffee.

On Friday, while the children were still here, we exchanged gifts. We had exchanged names among ourselves a week ago. Kermit put a big box on the wide kitchen window sill for the packages. Treva decorated it with twining evergreen branches ("to make it look Christmasy," she said) and soon it began to be filled with enticing, mysterious, and gaily wrapped packages. Emily was so excited she could hardly keep away from them, but she did obey our rule of not squeezing or handling the packages.

It turned out that Emily had a gift for everyone—not just the one whose name she had drawn. They were big and expensive gifts, too.

Tonight Kermit said he might have to sell a few head of cattle now, even before they're fattened up enough for market, to help with his Christmas expenses. But we received a lot, too, and we can use all the gifts we received.

A fresh snowfall has begun tonight, and after the chores were done, Kermit, Emily, and I went for an enchanting walk in the moonlight with big, soft flakes of snow drifting down all around us. *Silent night . . . Holy night . . . All is calm . . . All is bright.*

December 30

More snow is coming down; we're sure having our share of it this winter—so much that Kermit can't keep after with shoveling. There's a big driveway here, and when the township snowplow passes by, Kermit wishes the driver would kindly swerve in our drive and out again; but of course, it's only wishful thinking. Chuck was at Little Falls and said people were out with their snow blowers or snow throwers, opening drives and walkways with little effort on their part. It looks like magic.

Kermit was shoveling by hand this morning and I was planning to help as soon as I had the dishes done, when a "Good Samaritan" came to our aid. A Jeep with a blade in front came roaring in our driveway, making the snow fly about as merrily as a snow thrower (and much more heartily) and had the drive cleared in short order! On seeing Kermit, with a friendly wave of his hand, the driver came over to exchange a few words. It was the oldest Bentley boy! When Kermit thanked him and wanted to pay him, he refused to take anything.

He said, "Happy New Year!" and with a big smile roared off again. It really is amazing how those boys have done an about face. Wonders never cease! We're sure glad that their misconceptions about our tax evasions have been cleared up. That certainly (and understandably) must have rankled them. It is probably true what Pop once said, that most disagreements and fall-outs between neighbors arise from misunderstandings. It sure makes you feel lighthearted when they are straightened out.

January 1

A brand new year, not yet marred by sins and mistakes, with a fresh chance to do better and to overcome our faults and inconsistencies. We are invited over to Ben and Rachel's house today for a pork and sauerkraut dinner, then we'll make a big supply of potato chips and divide them among us. The homemade ones are much better than store-bought and it's fun to get together to make them.

Later, before we left to go to Ben's, the owner of Tall Cedars Homestead stopped in and gave us the devastating news that we will have to move by April 1. His married son wants to move here and manage the farm. Whew! Just three months to find another farm! We were in a daze as we drove to Ben and Rachel's, discussing our possibilities.

At Ben's, we broke the news to them, and they immediately cheered us up by telling us of a farm for rent—a farm named Beechwood Acres. It's owned by Mrs. Elegant, the lady who gave us the little ferret.

We drove there immediately to look at it and to negotiate the rent. It is a nice place and I think I would like to live there. Mrs. Elegant showed us around. It's nice, the land is good, and the rent reasonable. All we have to do is decide; she wants to know within two weeks. We'll have to talk it over and pray about it.

January 8

Emily's little pet ferret Mini hasn't been well of late. Yesterday she took a turn for the worse, so she was taken to the vet.

Emily's parents brought her this morning and had Mini along in her box, looking very sick. By the expression on their faces, I knew that the prognosis wasn't good. Emily's mother purposely asked Emily to show her the horses in the barn. Emily eagerly took her to see them while her dad explained to us about the ferret's illness.

Mr. Simmons used several big names or words that I can't remember, but what it amounts to is that Mini has an obstruction somewhere and needs to have surgery if she is to live. It will cost several thousand dollars, and at this time he won't be able to foot such a bill. He said he hopes we will be able to pay to have it done, for Emily's sake; otherwise, the ferret will have to be put to sleep.

Kermit slowly shook his head. I knew he was thinking, *Spend several thousand dollars on a ferret? For all we know, she might be old and about to die anyway.* But he didn't put it into words.

Before Emily's dad left, he said, "Well, think it over. If you decide to go ahead with it, she'll have to be at the animal hospital by one o'clock. Call me, and I'll take her in. All you would have to do would be to sell a couple of quilts." With that, he went out the door.

It was a rough forenoon, with Emily being all teary over her sick pet and we having the burden of being asked to foot the bill when we didn't think we could afford it, and not knowing if we would be good stewards of our money even if we could have scraped together that much. But then, at eleven o'clock, we received a big surprise along with the answer to our dilemma.

There was a knock on the door and there on the porch stood Mrs. Elegant. I invited her to stay for dinner and she accepted my invitation.

When we told her the story of Emily's little pet and the costly surgery that was necessary, Mrs. Elegant told us to by all means go ahead with it and she would gladly pay for it. So that's what we did and it sure was a load off our minds.

Mrs. Elegant said she had been hoping we would have shoo-fly pie for dinner. Since we didn't, right after dinner I started mixing dough to make some. She sat on a chair and watched while I rolled out the dough and prepared the filling and crumbs, chatting all the while. Then I took her on a tour of the farm. She said it was really interesting, even though she had to brave the wintry weather.

Later, Kermit and I talked about our renting her Beechwood Acres farm. We could tell that she would be delighted, but we will have to talk it over some more before we decide.

We really appreciated her coming because it turned out to be a good day after all. We sent a shoo-fly pie home with her and invited her to come back as often as she can.

Emily is happy again and when her mom came for her tonight, she said Mini came through the surgery and is on the road to recovery. Kermit and I decided a bit of celebrating was in order.

Kermit took the axe to the creek and chopped a sack full of ice chips to use in the hand-crank ice cream freezer. I prepared the custard for Oreo cookie ice cream and he cranked it. It was a cold but delicious treat for the wintertime. We sat by the fire and talked, counting our blessings, trying not to think about the decision we'll have to make regarding where to move and the uncertainty of what we'll do.

Jared and Treva had gone sledding with Joey Bentley and Bethany Bryan, so we had the evening to ourselves. When they came trooping in, I made hot chocolate, and they all wanted homemade ice cream even though it was cold.

January 12

The young folks—Treva, Jared, Joey, and Bethany—have gone skating tonight. I expect they'll soon come in to take turns warming their feet in the Gem-Pak oven. Kermit is putting a cedar chest together. I should be quilting, but I decided to rest my tired back for a few minutes while I add an entry to my journal.

Emily had a happy day today—her beloved Mini came home from the vet. The ferret is much improved, though she prefers to spend most of the time in her box. She can eat again and, according to the vet, should be good as new soon. Emily spent most of the day hovering around Mini's box, stroking her gently with her fingertips and crooning words of affection to her. All that TLC should help her to get better fast.

Emily asked me what the Dutch word is for Mini. I had to think awhile about that, but then remembered that mini means "little," and the Dutch word for little is *glah*. Soon Emily was saying, "*Glah* Mini, *Glah* Mini," over and over in a lilting, sing-song voice until she sang the ferret to sleep.

I hope that when and if we move, Emily's mother will consent to taking Mini on a permanent basis. She's used to having the run of the house and wouldn't be very happy in a cage. I am hoping that we'll be moving to Mrs. Elegant's place.

January 15

Well, I guess it's settled. We'll be moving to Beechwood Acres in March if all goes as planned! But that means we'll be leaving Tall Cedars Homestead and Treva, Jared, and Emily. Emily's mom says she will find another babysitter, since it would be too far for her to drive every day. I know the parting will be hard, but we have a lot of good memories to take along. It will tug at my heartstrings to move away from our Tall Cedars Homestead, but such is life. We won't be closer to my parents, but we'll still be able to write to each other and we'll be close to Mom and Pop Mullet.

What will become of our little Emily? We will miss her so much. I'll always remember her in my prayers.

I'd better get busy soon and start packing our household goods and wedding gifts we'll be taking along. I hope we'll have as many good memories when we leave Beechwood Acres as we do of Tall Cedars Homestead. Then again, there are some not-so-good memories—such as the time someone set fire to our peepie house. But all's well that ends well.

February 14

Valentine's Day! Only three more weeks at Tall Cedars Homestead, since we've set the moving day for March 7. Emily begged us to make valentines, so I stopped working on the last quilt I intend to make here, and we sat at the table with a supply of red construction paper, white paper lace, glue, and scissors. We made one for Emily's mother and dad, one for my parents and all the family, one for Kermit's mom, and one for the Mullets. Mini scampered around on the table playing with paper scraps. She's as frisky and energetic as ever, thanks to Mrs. Elegant.

I made a valentine for Kermit and put on this verse:

Love is patient,
Love is kind.
I am your valentine,
And I'm so glad you're mine.

I hid it under the stack of books on the desk, intending to give it later. When Kermit came in, he got involved in valentine making, too. He cut out a red heart, glued lace all around it, and also wrote a verse on it. Before he was quite finished with it, the feed man drove in the lane and Kermit had to leave. He put it in his pocket and said he would finish it later. I guess I'll have to be patient.

Now Emily is begging to go for a walk, and I think we will. It's a mild, spring-like day, quite welcome after the cold snap we had. While hanging out the wash this morning, I heard a song sparrow singing, and from the marsh I heard a red-winged blackbird calling, "Kong-a-ree! Spring is coming!" I'm longing to be able to find enough fresh dandelion for a meal. Spring seems to be coming earlier this year and I'm glad we'll be able to enjoy a bit of it in both places. We'll probably have quite a few days of cold and snow yet, but it doesn't hurt to dream of springtime.

February 16

Emily's parents have consented to take both Mini and Snickers when we move. That is a load off my mind. Our mild weather continues and we're getting eager to go for a walk up in Rocky Ridge before we leave. If the weather remains nice, perhaps we can do that on Sunday.

February 18 (Sunday)

This afternoon, the Mullets hosted a farewell singing for us as friends and relatives gathered at their place for a hymn sing.

It was heartwarming to us, and I tried to impress the memory of their kind and friendly faces in my mind to take with us. It might be a long time until we see some of them again, especially Art and Delphine and Chuck. I'm glad we had this year at Tall Cedars Homestead, for it was surely worthwhile, even though we have to leave sooner than planned.

Our packing is all finished (except what we need before we move), and we're getting excited about moving. We're glad now that we kept our furnishings simple, since there's a lot less work in moving this way.

February 28

We were invited to the Bryans for supper last night. Since Emily was invited, too, her mom said she would pick her up later in the evening.

Walking up the trail in Rocky Ridge, we stopped to admire the rivulets of water which are flowing again, fed by the melted snow. The little pool under the waterfall was overflowing, and a few snow flowers were blooming beside it. While we stood there admiring it, Mr. and Mrs. Bentley passed us, giving us a friendly nod and wave of the hand. Later, the boys passed us on their ATV and were just as respectful and friendly. I'm glad we aren't leaving Tall Cedars with them still mad at us!

Emily seemed to be bubbling over with some secret and kept urging us on, wanting us to go faster. We were met on the porch by a smiling Mrs. Bryan and Bethany. They ushered us inside and down the stairs to the basement. Throwing open the door, Bethany cried, "Surprise! Surprise!" And Emily gleefully joined in.

We sure were surprised to see the room full of our friends—Kermit's mom, the Mullets, Chuck, Art and Delphine, Jill and Wynn, Ben and Rachel. In the middle of the room Emily eagerly pulled us over to a big box full of gaily wrapped packages. "A sunshine box full of gifts for you!" she said happily.

"An ABC box," Bethany said. "You take it along to your new home, and you can open only one package a day! That's to keep you from getting homesick."

Kermit and I were simply overwhelmed, and we felt quite unworthy of all the attention we were getting. I guess you might have called it a farewell party, for they sang farewell songs such as "God Be With You Till We Meet Again" and "Some Sweet Day" (about a place where parted friends know no farewells and tears are wiped away). Truly that will be a happy time, some sweet day.

Emily wanted us to open all the packages right away, but that would've done away with the pleasant anticipation of opening a package a day after we moved. The supper was "covered dish" (delicious) and after the dishes were washed, we visited until late in the evening. After we move we won't have this privilege so we'll try to cherish the memory of the kindness of our friends and all they've done for us. What would we do without kind and caring friends to help us in times of need?

March 6

Today was Emily's last day with us, and tonight she cried heartbrokenly when she hugged me goodbye. She soon forgot her sadness, though, in the joy of taking Mini and Snickers along home. Her parents haven't found another babysitter yet, but they have a few prospects, and they'll keep on looking until they find one.

Jared took Treva home on the pony cart tonight, then drove on out to his home. Our belongings are all loaded for the trip, thanks to the help of our kind friends and neighbors. We're taking our wedding gifts, and the basics we'll need to set up housekeeping at Beechwood Acres. Chuck will keep the Gem-Pak, since there is a cookstove waiting for us in the "new" house. I'm so eager to see it all again.

We took a tour of Tall Cedars Homestead tonight, I guess to say goodbye. The barn is empty—Silver and Patsy, Dick and Daisy, and Bossy have already been moved to the farm. The cats and the Bantys were here when we came and will go to the next farmer.

A robin was hopping about in the barnyard, the spring flowering bulbs along the fence were pushing green shoots, and the grass was turning green. It sure did tug at our heartstrings to be leaving it all—our first home together. Our homey little cabin, the tall cedars where the wind sighs soothingly, and the surrounding trees all seemed very dear as we thought of leaving them permanently. The rose arbor Kermit made for me is loaded on the truck, but the rosebush he gave me for my birthday will be left behind.

We gazed fondly at the old cedar trees, the meadow with its winding little river, the wooded hillside that connects to Rocky Ridge, the cattle in the meadow, and the old waterwheel. Tomorrow we will leave it all, bound for new adventures on Beechwood Acres farm! A new chapter of our lives will unfold. Mom has given me a new journal to fill, since there are only a few more pages left in this one. Time will tell, as to whether or not I'll get it filled.

Mom had included a letter that she had received from a minister's wife from here in the Swift River Settlement. In it were a few words about us. It brought tears to my eyes as I read it. I'll copy it here:

> *Kermit is a fine young man and Joy seems to be just the wife for him. The ministers say that, considering the upbringing he had, he is doing remarkably well and seems to be growing in his spiritual life. They seem to be well-adjusted to each other, practicing tolerance and forbearance in overlooking each other's faults, and nurturing love. I suppose it must have been quite an adjustment for them that first year, with their different backgrounds.*

Hmmm . . . I wonder how they knew so much about us, and whether we deserve all that praise.

March 7

We arrived at Beechwood Acres today and had a rather busy and hectic day, getting everything in place. But we had a lot of good helpers, and by this evening everything was done and we were settled in our new home.

Mom Mullet brought our dinner over in the spring wagon and soon had a fire going in the cookstove, making the kitchen warm and cheery and filled with a good aroma.

After the menfolk had all the furniture in place, we women did the rest—hanging curtains, making the beds, and unpacking the dishes and things to put in the cupboards. Rachel and I added homey touches here and there, selecting items Kermit and I had received as wedding gifts—rugs, cushions, a few mottoes and knickknacks, and wall calendars. Now all it needs are our cheery houseplants which are still in Chuck's bunkhouse.

This evening, after everyone had left, Kermit and I felt almost overwhelmed by all everyone had done for us and all the kindness they have shown. Now it's up to us to remember to return and pass on all the favors. Time to quit writing now, since we have a busy day planned for tomorrow. I'll copy one more Golden Gem in this diary:

Praising and believing are one. There must be a continual repetition of the act of faith, cleaving fast to the Word of God until He bestows the blessing.

March 9

Only one more page to fill in this journal. Kermit and I took a walk through the "bushland" tonight, just as the sun was setting in a maze of red and pink glory over the Beechwood trees, reflecting in the pond until it glowed with color and brightness. It was one of the loveliest sunsets we had ever seen. I tried to imagine how lovely it will be when the fruit trees are in blossom with the sweet, fragrant pink and white petals floating down with the breeze, and the air ringing with the melody of birdsong. The only things that might surpass the beauty of tonight might be climbing rose bushes in blossom with their clouds of sweet fragrance wafting in the breeze and he blooming honeysuckle vines climbing the trellis.

Our sojourn on Beechwood Acres has begun, and we wonder what the year may bring. We know we'll be busy, and we hope that our days will hold enough joys to keep us happy, and enough trials to keep us humble. We'll work and plan and dream while following God's leading as hand-in-hand through life we go.

Twilight is descending and Kermit is coming in with the horses now, but there is time for one last verse of "Love At Home":

Jesus show Thy mercy mine, Then there's love at home.
Sweetly whisper, I am Thine, Then there's love at home.
Source of love, Thy cheering light, Far exceeds the sun so bright,
Can dispel the gloom of night, Then there's love at home!